D0513906

AUTHOR	CLASS
NASH. J	822.91
TITLE	No.
Rainmaker	2984690

LANCASHIRE COUNTY COUNCIL

This book should be returned on or before the latest date
shown above to the library from which it was borrowed

LIBRARY HEADQUARTERS, 143 CORPORATION STREET, PRESTON, PR1 8RH

THE RAINMAKER

A Comedy in Three Acts

by

N. RICHARD NASH

LONDON
SAMUEL FRENCH LIMITED

SAMUEL FRENCH LTD
26 SOUTHAMPTON STREET, STRAND, LONDON, W.C.2

SAMUEL FRENCH INC.
25 WEST 45TH STREET, NEW YORK, U.S.A.
7623 SUNSET BOULEVARD, HOLLYWOOD 46, CAL.

SAMUEL FRENCH (CANADA) LTD
27 GRENVILLE STREET, TORONTO

SAMUEL FRENCH (AUSTRALIA) PTY LTD
159 FORBES STREET, SYDNEY

MADE AND PRINTED IN GREAT BRITAIN BY
BUTLER & TANNER LTD, FROME AND LONDON

MADE IN ENGLAND

THE RAINMAKER

Produced at St Martin's Theatre, London, on the 31st May 1956, with the following cast of characters—

(in the order of their appearance)

H. C. CURRY	*Wilfrid Lawson*
NOAH CURRY, his elder son	*Gordon Tanner*
JIM CURRY, his younger son	*Neil McCallum*
LIZZIE CURRY, his daughter	*Geraldine Page*
FILE	*Michael Goodliffe*
SHERIFF THOMAS	*Launce Maraschal*
BILL STARBUCK	*Sam Wanamaker*

Directed by JACK MINSTER and SAM WANAMAKER

Setting by RALPH ALSWANG

Set Adaptation by MICHAEL NORTHEN

SYNOPSIS OF SCENES

The action of the play passes in a Western State of the U.S.A. on a Summer day in a time of drought

ACT I

Day

ACT II

That evening

ACT III

Later the same night

All applications for a licence to perform this play, both by amateur and professional companies must be made to us, or to our authorized agents.

The fee for one performance of this play by amateurs is Five Guineas, payable in advance to us, or to our authorized agents.

Upon payment of the fee a licence will be issued for the performance to take place. No performance may be given unless this licence has first been obtained.

In the event of further performances being given, the fee for each and every performance subsequent to the first is Four Guineas. This reduction applies only in the case of the performances being **consecutive** and at the **same theatre or hall.**

The following particulars are needed for the issue of a licence:

    Title of the play
    Name of the town
    Name of the theatre or hall
    Date of the performance(s)
    Name and address of the applicant
    Name of the society

Please state the amount remitted with the application.

The fee for performance by professional companies will be quoted on application.

SAMUEL FRENCH LTD
26 Southampton Street
Strand, London, W.C.2

Character costumes and wigs used in the performance of plays contained in French's Acting Edition may be obtained from Messrs CHARLES H. FOX Ltd, 184 High Holborn, London, W.C.1

Photograph by Houston Rogers

THE RAINMAKER

ACT I

SCENE—*The living-room on the Curry ranch in a Western State of the U.S.A. Early morning on a Summer day in a time of drought.*

The setting is composite with the living-room C, File's office R and the tack-room L. The Curry ranch is a prosperous one and the house is a place where gentle, kindly people who have an uneducated but profoundly true sense of beauty have lived in love of one another. It is strongly masculine in its basic structure, brick and hand-hewn beams and such, but it shows Lizzie's hand in many of its appointments. We see a kitchen L; the rest of the downstairs living area is a combination of living- and dining-room. The front door is R giving on to a porch and thence to the private road that leads to the main highway. There are stairs leading up and off L to the bedrooms. There are windows back C, up R and in the kitchen. A dining-table stands up C with four chairs around it. A fifth chair is L of the window up C. Down L is a settee with a hassock in front of it. A long, low linen chest is down R. In the corner up R there is a table with a primitive crystal radio set hooked up to an old phonograph horn. There is a Dutch dresser up L. An early type of telephone is fixed to a wall beam L. At night the room is lit by an oil lamp suspended C and an oil lamp in a bracket fixed to the beam over the telephone. In the kitchen there is a sink and cooking utensils on the shelves. In File's office down R there is an ancient roll-top desk with an old style telephone on it; a swivel chair; a stool and a well-worn leather couch. On the wall is a bulletin board with various "Wanted" posters featuring the faces of criminals. The walls are warmly stained knotty pine. There is a window R overlooking the street, with an entrance above it. At night, the room is lit by a goose-neck lamp on the desk. The tack-room down L is a rough, picturesque room, a junk room, really. A slanting ceiling with huge hand-hewn beams; a wagon wheel against a wall; leather goods, saddles, horse traces and the like; sacks of feed; tools; a buggy seat and a nail keg. A farm lantern hangs from a nail. It is a room altogether accidental, yet altogether romantic. The door is at the back and the window is L.

(See the Ground Plan and Photograph of the Scene)

When the CURTAIN *rises, the* LIGHTS *come up on the living-room, leaving the office and tack-room in darkness. It is early morning of a scorching, drought-ridden day. Already the blazing sun has taken over the house. A suitcase stands behind the settee and various gifts and wrappings are scattered on the floor* LC *and on the settee; a fountain pen,*

*a horsehair hat-band and a tooled leather belt with a large shiny buckle.
H. C. CURRY is in the kitchen, preparing breakfast. He is in his mid-fifties, powerfully set, capable, a good man to take store in. But he is not all prosaic efficiency, there is a dream in him. He wears an apron. After a moment, NOAH CURRY, his elder son, enters R. He is somewhat like his father, but without H.C.'s imagination. As a matter of fact, he has little imagination at all; a somewhat self-righteous man, rigidly opinionated. He carries a saddle.*

NOAH. That you, Pop?

H.C. Yeah. Mornin', Noah.

NOAH. I heard somebody fussin' around in the kitchen—I was hopin' it was Lizzie. (*He puts the saddle on the floor down R beside the chest*)

H.C. (*coming into the room*) She was so dead beat after her trip I figured I'd let her sleep.

NOAH. Yeah. I heard her walkin' her room last night until Hell knows when. (*He looks at his pocket watch*) Gettin' late. Maybe I better wake her up. (*He starts for the stairs*)

H.C. (*moving to the dresser*) No—don't do that, Noah. (*He takes a tablecloth from the dresser and spreads it on the table*) She must of had a pretty rough time. Let her sleep it off. (*He goes to the dresser and transfers jam, cruet, bread, etc. to the table*)

NOAH. I was sure hopin' she'd cook breakfast. (*Quickly, with a half smile, so as not to offend H.C.*) But I guess if we didn't croak after a week of your cookin', we can live through another meal. (*He goes to the radio and fiddles with it*)

(*The radio screeches*)

H.C. Noah—Jimmy just fixed that thing—don't you go breakin' it again.

NOAH. If that kid's gonna waste his money on a darn-fool crystal set—why can't we get some good out of it? Can't hear a thing.

H.C. (*moving to the dresser*) What do you want to hear? (*He transfers four mugs and the cutlery to the table and sets them out*)

NOAH. Thought somebody'd say somethin' about the drought.

H.C. Only one thing to say. No rain.

NOAH (*switching off the radio*) And no sign of it, neither. (*He goes to the calendar on the wall, R of the window up C*) Well, cross out another day. (*He marks a day off the calendar*)

H.C. Noah, I wish you wouldn't do that. (*He moves to the kitchen door*) You and that damn calendar. Why'n't you stop countin'. When it rains, it rains. (*He goes into the kitchen*)

NOAH. You know what I seen this mornin'. (*He crosses to the dresser and takes two ledgers from the cupboard*) Three more calves down and out—and a couple of heifers. And you know what I had to do? I had to give Sandy and Frank their time.

(H.C. *comes from the kitchen. He carries a jug of milk, which he puts on the table*)

H.C. (*disturbed*) You mean you fired them?

NOAH. No—I just laid 'em off—till the drought's over.

H.C. You shouldn't of done that, Noah.

NOAH. Listen, Pop—if you want to take over the book-keepin', you're welcome to it. (*He puts the ledgers on the dresser*) Here's the books—you can have 'em. (*He crosses to R of the table*)

H.C. (*moving to L of the table; with a smile*) Now I wouldn't do that to you, Noah. How do you want your eggs?

NOAH. What's the best way you can't ruin 'em?

H.C. Raw. (*He takes a plate from the dresser and goes into the kitchen*)

NOAH (*crossing to the hassock and sitting*) I'll take 'em raw.

(JIM CURRY *comes racing downstairs. He is the youngest in the family, in his early twenties, but he is big and broad-shouldered and looks older until he opens his mouth, then he is a child. He is not very bright and this is his great cross. He is filled with inchoate longing. At the moment he is agog with excitement, as he nearly always is, but right now his frenzy has to do with universal catastrophe. He carries his shoes*)

JIM. Mornin'. Mornin', Pop.

H.C. } (*together*) {Mornin', Jimmy.
NOAH }   {Mornin'.

JIM (*moving down* C) Pop! Pop, it's like I said yesterday—just like I told you.

H.C. What'd you tell me, Jim?

JIM (*putting on his shoes*) I said to you like this, I said: "Pop, the whole world's gonna blow up." I said: "The world's gonna get all s-w-o-l-e up—and bust right in our faces."

H.C. You sure of that, Jimmy?

JIM. You bet I'm sure. You see, it's all got to do with the spots on the sun. One of these days them spots is gonna get so big the sun won't be able to shine through. (*He crosses to the porch*) And then, brother—bang!

(H.C. *comes from the kitchen. He carries a plate with two raw eggs.* NOAH *rises, takes the plate from H.C. and sits R of the table*)

NOAH. You keep thinkin' about that you're gonna miss your breakfast.

JIM (*crossing to* C) Yeah. Ain't no good thinkin' about it—it just gets me all upset. (*He sits L of the table and notices Noah's food*) Holy mackerel, Noah—them eggs is raw. (*He starts to gorge on bread and jam*)

NOAH. What of it?

JIM. What's the matter—you sick?

NOAH. No, I ain't sick.

JIM. You sure must be sick if you're eating raw eggs.

H.C. (*moving above the table*) He's all right, Jim. He just don't like my cookin'.

JIM. Why? You cook better'n Lizzie. I like the way you cook, Pop. Everything slides down nice and greasy.

H.C. (*wryly accepting the dubious compliment*) Thanks, Jim. How do you want your eggs? (*He takes two plates from the dresser and goes into the kitchen*)

JIM. Oh, any old way.

H.C. How many?

JIM (*casually*) I guess five or six'll do.

NOAH. Jimmy . . .

JIM (*bolting his food; not looking up*) Huh?

NOAH. Jimmy, if you'll come up for a minute, I got somethin' to say to you.

JIM. What?

NOAH. Last night—you coulda got yourself into a hatful of trouble.

(H.C. *comes from the kitchen*)

JIM (*embarrassed to discuss it in front of his father*) Do we have to talk about it now?

H.C. What kind of trouble, Noah?

NOAH (*distastefully*) A certain girl named Snookie.

H.C. (*moving above the settee*) Oh—was Snookie at the dance?

NOAH. Was she at the dance! You'd a thought nobody else was there. She comes drivin' up in a brand-new five-cylinder Essex car. And her hair is so bleach-blonde . . .

JIM. It ain't bleached.

NOAH. Don't tell me! Gil Demby says she comes into the store and buys a pint of peroxide every month.

JIM. What's that? I use peroxide for a cut finger.

NOAH. If she got cut that often she'd bleed to death.

H.C. (*quietly*) What happened, Jim?

NOAH. I'll tell you what happened. Along about nine-thirty I look around. No Jim—and no Snookie. That dumb kid—he walked outta that barn dance without even tippin' his hat.

(H.C. *goes into the kitchen, takes off his apron and hangs it up*)

And he went off with that hot pants girl.

JIM. I didn't go off with her—I went off by myself. I walked outside and I was lookin' at that Essex. And pretty soon she comes out and she's kinda starin' me up and down. And I says to her: "How many cylinders has this Essex got?" And she says: "Five." And then she says to me: "How tall are you?" And I says: "Six." And before you know it we're ridin' in the Essex and she's got that car racin' forty miles an hour. Man, it was fast.

NOAH. Everything about her is fast.

JIM (*rearing*) Whatta you mean by that, Noah?

(*H.C. comes from the kitchen. He carries two plates of scrambled eggs which he puts on the table*)

NOAH. Just what I said.

(*H.C. sits above the table. During the ensuing speeches the three men eat their breakfast*)

When the dance was over—when we were all supposed to go pick Lizzie up at the depot—I had to go lookin' for him. And you know where he was? He was sittin' in that girl's car—parked outside of Demby's store—and the two of them—I never saw such carryin's on. They were so twisted up together, I couldn't tell where he left off and Snookie began. If I hadn't of come along, hell knows what would of happened.

JIM (*tragically*) Yeah—hell knows—I could of come home with her little red hat.

H.C. With her what?

NOAH. She wears a little red hat.

H.C. Well, why would you come home with her little red hat?

JIM. Nothin'—nothin'.

NOAH. Go on—tell him.

JIM. Noah—you quit it.

NOAH. Well, I'll tell him. She always wears this little red hat. And last night, Dumbo Hopkinson says to her: "Snookie, you gonna wear that little red hat all your life?" And she giggles and says: "Well, I hope not, Dumbo. I'm gonna give it to some handsome fella—when, as and if."

(*H.C. smiles*)

It ain't funny, Pop. (*To Jim*) Do you know what trouble you can get yourself into with a girl like that? A dumb kid like you—why, pretty soon she's got you hog-tied and you have to marry her.

JIM. Why don't you let me alone?

NOAH (*outraged*) Did you hear that, Pop?

H.C. Maybe it's a good idea, Noah.

NOAH. What's a good idea?

H.C. To let him alone.

JIM. Maybe it is.

(*NOAH rises and goes into the kitchen*)

NOAH (*hurt; in high dudgeon*) All right! If you want me to let you alone—Kid, you're alone.

JIM (*withdrawing a little*) I don't know what you're gettin' so mad about.

(*NOAH comes in from the kitchen, carrying a pot of coffee*)

NOAH. You don't, huh? (*He pours the coffee*) You think I like lookin' out for you? Well, I don't. Taggin' after me all your life. "How do I tie my shoelaces? How do I do long divisions?" Well, if you don't want me to give you no advice—if you think you're so smart . . .

JIM. I ain't sayin' I'm so smart. Heck, I don't mind you tellin' me how to do and how to figure things out . . .

NOAH (*bitingly*) Thanks! (*He sits* R *of the table*)

JIM. What I mean—I appreciate it. (*He bellows*) I just wish you wouldn't holler.

H.C. (*rising*) All right—that's enough, boys.

(*There is a pause. H.C. goes on to the porch and looks at the thermometer*)

A hundred and one degrees.

NOAH. If only it'd cool off at night.

JIM (*rising and moving to the foot of the stairs*) I don't mind a hot night. (*Longingly*) Somethin' about a hot night—gets you kind of —well—all stirred up inside. Why didn't Lizzie come down and make our breakfast, Pop? (*He sits on the hassock*)

H.C. Let her sleep. She didn't sleep much last night.

JIM. Yeah. Gets off the train—comes home—and starts cleanin' up her bedroom in the middle of the night. Hell, there was no need for that, I cleaned her room up real nice.

H.C. (*quietly*) Jimmy, when some girls ain't happy they cry—Lizzie works. (*He moves to the chest and sits on it*)

JIM. Yeah. Well, what are we gonna do about her?

H.C. (*worriedly*) I don't know.

JIM. We gotta do somethin', Pop. We gotta at least talk to her. Mention.

H.C. Who's gonna mention it to her?

NOAH. I told you, Pop—I'm not gonna talk to her.

JIM. Me, neither. I'm not gonna talk to her.

H.C. Stop sayin' exactly what Noah's sayin'. Speak for yourself.

JIM. I say what Noah is sayin' because I agree with him. When I don't, I spit in his eye.

H.C. Then why won't you talk to her?

JIM. Because if we do, she'll think we're tryin' to get rid of her.

H.C. She'll sure think the same if I do it.

NOAH. Maybe.

JIM. Maybe.

H.C. So there you are.

JIM. But you're her father and comes a time when a father's gotta mention.

H.C. I can't. I can't just speak up and say: "Lizzie, you gotta get married." She know she's gotta get married. We all know it.

(*The sound of a door slam is heard off upstairs*)

NOAH. Well, then—seems there's no point to mention anything.

(LIZZIE CURRY *enters down the stairs. At first glance, she seems a woman who can cope with all the aspects of her life. She has the world of materiality under control; she is a good housekeeper; pots and pans, needles and thread—when she touches them, they serve. She knows well where she fits in the family—she is daughter, sister, mother, child—and she enjoys the manifold elements of her position. She has a sure ownership of her own morality, for the tenets of right and wrong are friendly to her—and she is comfortably forthright in living by them. A strong and integral woman in every life function—except one. Here she is, twenty-seven years old, and no man outside the family has loved her or found her beautiful. And yet, ironically, it is this one unfulfilled part of Lizzie that is the most potentially beautiful facet of the woman—this yearning for romance—this courageous searching for it in the desert of her existence—and if some day a man should find her, he will find a ready woman, willing to give herself with the totality of her rich being*)

LIZZIE. Morning, Pop. (*She crosses to* C) Noah—Jimmy. (*She moves to the settee, picks up the belt and puts it on*)

H.C. Mornin', honey.

NOAH } (*together*) { Mornin', Lizzie.
JIM } { Hi, Liz.

LIZZIE. Sure good to be home again.

H.C. Just what the boys were sayin'—sure good to have Lizzie home again.

LIZZIE (*crossing to the porch*) No sign of rain yet, is there? (*She gazes out for a moment*)

H.C. Not a cloud nowhere.

LIZZIE. I dreamed we had a rain—a great big rain.

H.C. Did you, Lizzie?

LIZZIE. Thunderstorm. Rain coming down in sheets. (*She crosses to* C) Lightning flashed—thunder rolled up and down the canyon like a kid with a big drum. I looked up and I laughed and yelled. (*She crosses to the door* R. *With a laugh*) Oooh, it was wonderful!

NOAH. Drought's drought—and a dream's a dream.

LIZZIE. But it was a nice dream, Noah—and nearly as good as rain.

NOAH. Near ain't rain.

H.C. It's too bad we picked you up at the depot so late last night, Lizzie. Didn't have much time to talk about your trip.

NOAH. Looks like it perked you up real good. Yeah, you were lookin' all dragged out by the heat. What was it like in Sweetriver?

LIZZIE (*moving to* L *of the table*) Hotter'n hell.

(H.C. *and* JIM *laugh*)

NOAH. I don't see nothin' funny in her talkin' like a cowhand.

LIZZIE. Sorry, Noah. That's about all the conversation I've heard for a week.

H.C. How's Uncle Ned, Lizzie? And Aunt Ivy?

JIM. And how's all them boys?

LIZZIE. Big.

H.C. If they take after Aunt Ivy I bet they talked your ear off.

LIZZIE. No, they take after Uncle Ned. They just grunt.

NOAH. Who got to be the best lookin' of the boys, Lizzie?

LIZZIE (*moving down* LC) Oh, I guess Pete.

H.C. Never could get those boys straight. Which one is Pete?

LIZZIE. He's the one with the yellow hair.

NOAH (*quickly*) Yella hair's nice in a man.

JIM. It's honest.

LIZZIE. Oh, Pete was honest all right.

JIM. The way you said that I bet you liked him the best.

LIZZIE. Oh, I'm crazy about Pete—he asked me to marry him.

H.C. (*after a pause*) Is that true, Lizzie?

JIM (*rising; agog*) He did! What did you tell him?

LIZZIE. I told him I would—as soon as he graduates from Grammar School.

(*There is a silence*)

JIM. Grammar School! Is he that dumb?

LIZZIE (*with a laugh*) No, he's only nine years old.

(*There is a pause.* JIM *moves to the window up* C)

(*Seeing the stricken look on their faces, she moves down* L) Pop, let's not beat around the bush. I know why you sent me to Sweetriver. Because Uncle Ned's got six boys. Three of them are old enough to get married—and so am I. Well, I'm sorry you went to all that expense—the railroad ticket—all those new clothes—the trip didn't work. Noah, you can write it in the books—in red ink.

H.C. What happened at Sweetriver, Lizzie?

LIZZIE (*emptily*) Nothing—not a doggone thing.

H.C. What did you do? Where'd you go?

(LIZZIE *kneels by her suitcase, opens it and tidies the garments in it*)

LIZZIE. Well, the first three or four days I was there—I stayed in my room most of the time.

NOAH. What'd you do that for?

LIZZIE. Because I was embarrassed.

NOAH. Embarrassed about what?

LIZZIE. Noah, use your head. I knew what I was there for—and that whole family knew it, too. And I couldn't stand the way they were looking me over. So I'd go downstairs for my meals—and rush right back to my room. I packed—I unpacked—

I washed my hair a dozen times—I read the Sears, Roebuck catalogue from cover to cover. And finally, I said to myself: "Lizzie Curry, snap out of this." Well, it was a Saturday night —and they were all going to a rodeo dance. So I got myself all decked out in my highest heels and my lowest cut dress. And I walked down to that supper table and all those boys looked at me as if I was stark naked. And then for the longest while there wasn't a sound at the table except for Uncle Ned slupping his soup. And then suddenly—like a gunshot—I heard Ned junior say: "Lizzie, how much do you weigh?"

H.C. What'd you say to that?

LIZZIE (*rising*) I said, "I weigh a hundred and nineteen pounds, my teeth are all my own and I stand seventeen hands high."

NOAH. That wasn't very smart of you, Lizzie. He was just trying to open the conversation.

LIZZIE (*picking up the suitcase; wryly*) Well, I guess I closed it. (*She moves up L and puts the suitcase on the floor in the corner*) Then, about ten minutes later, little Pete came hurrying in to the supper table. He was carrying a geography book and he said: "Hey, Pop—where's Madagascar?" Well, everybody ventured an opinion and they were all dead wrong. And suddenly I felt I had to make a good impression, and I said: "It's an island in the India Ocean off the coast of Africa right opposite Mozambique."

(NOAH *groans*)

(*With a wail*) Can I help it if I was good in geography?

(JIM *crosses to the door* R)

H.C. What happened?

LIZZIE. Everything was so quiet it sounded like the end of the world. Then I heard Ned junior's voice: "Lizzie, you fixin' to be a schoolmarm?"

H.C. Oh, no!

LIZZIE (*moving to the hassock and sitting on it*) Yes. And suddenly I felt like I was way back at the high school dance—and nobody dancing with me. And I had a sick feeling that I was wearing glasses again the way I used to. And I knew from that minute on that it was no go. So I didn't go to the rodeo dance with them —I stayed home and made up poems about what was on sale at Sears, Roebuck's.

H.C. You and little Pete?

LIZZIE. Yes—and the day I left Sweetriver little Pete was bawling. And he said: "You're the beautifulest girl that ever was."

H.C. (*rising and crossing to Lizzie*) And he's right. You are.

LIZZIE (*with more pain than pleasure*) Oh, Pop, please!

H.C. We see you that way—he saw you that way.

LIZZIE. But not his big brothers.

H.C. Because you didn't show yourself right.

LIZZIE. I tried, Pop—I tried.

H.C. No, you didn't. You hid behind your books. You hid behind your glasses that you don't even wear no more. You're afraid of bein' beautiful.

(LIZZIE *rises and moves towards the kitchen*)

LIZZIE (*in an outburst*) I'm afraid to think I am when I know I'm not. (*She goes into the kitchen*)

(LIZZIE's *intensity stops the discussion. There is a pause.* NOAH *rises, crosses to the dresser and replaces the ledgers in the cupboard, then crosses to* RC)

H.C. (*calling*) Lizzie.

LIZZIE (*in the kitchen*) Yes?

H.C. (*moving* C) Me and the boys—we put our heads together and we thought we'd mention somethin' to you.

LIZZIE (*calling*) What?

H.C. (*to Noah; uncomfortably*) You want to tell her about it, Noah?

NOAH. Nope. It's your idea, Pop.

H.C. Well, the boys and me—after we get some work done—we figure to ride into Three Point this afternoon.

(LIZZIE *comes from the kitchen and stands* L *of the table*)

LIZZIE. Well?

H.C. We're goin' to the Sheriff's office and gonna talk to his deputy.

LIZZIE (*alert now*) File?

H.C. Yes—File.

LIZZIE. Pop, that's the craziest idea . . .

H.C. I'm just gonna invite him to supper, Lizzie.

LIZZIE. If you do, I won't be here.

H.C. I can invite a fella to supper in my own house, can't I?

LIZZIE. I don't want you to go out and lasso a husband for me.

H.C. I won't do anything of the kind. I won't even say your name. We'll start talkin' about a poker game maybe—and then we'll get around supper—and before you know it, he'll be sittin' right in that chair.

LIZZIE. No!

H.C. (*crossing to the settee*) Lizzie, we're goin'—no matter what you say. (*He picks up his hat from the settee and crosses to* RC)

NOAH (*moving to* R *of H.C.*) Hold on, Pop. I'm against this. But if Lizzie says it's okay to go down there and talk to File— I'll go right along with you. But one thing—we won't do it if Lizzie says no.

Lizzie. And that's what I say—no.

H.C. Don't listen to Noah. Every time you and Jim have to scratch your back, you turn and ask Noah.

Lizzie. Because he's the only sensible one around here, Pop. The three of us—we get carried away, and then . . .

H.C. (*interrupting hotly*) For once in your life—get carried away. It won't hurt you—not a bit.

Noah. That's the dumbest advice I ever heard.

H.C. What's so dumb about it?

Noah. It's a matter of pride.

(*As* Lizzie *turns away,* H.C. *sees her rejection of "pride" as a reason for not going through with the plan. Now he confronts her with the question*)

H.C. Is that why you say "no", Lizzie? Pride?

Lizzie (*moving above the settee; avoiding the confrontation*) Pop, if you want to invite somebody to supper—go ahead—but not File. He doesn't even know I'm on earth.

H.C. (*with a quiet smile*) He knows, Lizzie—he knows.

Lizzie. No, he doesn't. Whenever we ride into town, File's got a great big hello for you and Noah and Jim—but he's got nothing for me. He just barely sneaks his hat off his head—and that's all. He makes a point of ignoring me.

H.C. (*moving to* R *of Lizzie; quietly*) When a man makes a point of ignorin' you, he ain't ignorin' you at all.

(Lizzie *looks at* H.C.)

How about it, Lizzie? File for supper?

Lizzie (*moving down* LC; *in an outburst*) No—I don't like him—no—no!

H.C. If you don't really like him—one "no" is enough—and you can say it quiet.

Lizzie (*controlling herself; quietly and deliberately*) All right—I don't like him. I don't like the way he tucks his thumbs in his belt—and I don't like the way he always seems to be thinking deep thoughts.

H.C. (*secretly amused*) I thought you liked people with deep thoughts.

Lizzie (*crossing down* L) Not File.

(Jim *crosses to* C)

H.C. (*moving to* R *of Lizzie; gently and soberly*) Lizzie—when you were a kid—if I ever thought you were lyin'—I'd say to you: "Honest in truth?" And then you'd never lie. Well, I'm sayin' it now—you don't like File—honest in truth?

Lizzie (*flustered*) Oh, Pop—that's silly.

H.C. I asked you a question. Honest in truth?

Lizzie (*chattering evasively*) Pop, that's a silly childish game and all you'll get is a silly childish answer, and I refuse—I simply refuse to—to . . .

(JIM *crosses and exits* R)

(*She suddenly puts the brakes on. In an outburst*) Oh, for God's sake, go on and invite him.

H.C. (*with a whooping shout*) O-kaaay! Come on, boys.

H.C. *and* NOAH *exit quickly* R. LIZZIE, *for an instant, is unnerved and alarmed at what she has let herself in for. Then suddenly, her spirits rising with expectancy, she goes about clearing the breakfast dishes. When* LIZZIE *is happy she dances as she works.* LIZZIE *is dancing as—*

the LIGHTS *fade to* BLACK-OUT

The LIGHTS *come up on File's office* R, *leaving the living-room and tack-room in darkness. The office is empty for a moment, then* FILE *and* SHERIFF THOMAS *enter.* FILE'S *thumbs, as Lizzie described them, are tucked in his belt. He is a lean man, reticent, intelligent, in his late thirties. He smiles wryly at the world and at himself. Perhaps he is a little bitter; if so, his bitterness is leavened by a mischievous humour. He and the Sheriff are deep in argument. Actually, it is the* SHERIFF *who is arguing.* FILE *is detached, humouring the Sheriff's argument. The men are obviously fond of each other.*

SHERIFF. File—will you listen to me, File?

FILE. Look here, Sheriff. When I was dead broke, you lent me some money. When I needed a job, you made me your deputy. When I catch cold, you bring me a mustard plaster. And now you want to give me a dog. Well, I don't want a dog.

SHERIFF. I won't charge you nothin' for it, File.

FILE. You never charge me for anything. I don't want a dog.

SHERIFF. How do you know you don't want him until you see him?

FILE. Well—I seen dogs before.

SHERIFF. Not this one—he's different. I tell you, File—you see this little fella and you'll reach out and wanta hug him to death.

FILE (*humouring him*) Think I will, huh?

SHERIFF. Yes, you will. He's real lovin'. If you're sittin' in your bare feet, he'll come over and lick your big toe. And pretty soon, there he is—dead asleep—right across your feet. How about it, File?

FILE (*hesitating*) Well—that sounds real homey—but I'll do without him.

SHERIFF (*sitting on the stool*) File, you make me disgusted. It ain't right for you to shack up all by yourself—with a coffee-pot and a leather sofa. Especially once you been married. When you lose your wife, the nights get damn cold. And you gotta have somethin' warm up against your backside.

File (*sitting in the desk chair*) Well, last night was a hundred and four degrees.

Sheriff. All right—if you don't want the dog—if you're the kind of fella that don't like animals . . .

File (*amused*) I like animals, Sheriff.

Sheriff. If you liked animals, you'd have animals.

File. Oh, I've had 'em.

Sheriff (*disbelievingly*) I'll bet! What kind?

File. Well, back in Pedleyville—I went out and got myself a racoon.

Sheriff. A racoon ain't a dog.

File (*with a smile*) No—I guess it ain't. But I liked him. He was a crazy little fella—made me laugh.

Sheriff. Yeah? Whatever happened to him?

File. I don't know. One day he took to the woods and never came back, the little bastard.

Sheriff (*triumphantly*) There—see? Now can you figure a dog doin' that? No, sir! I tell you, File, if you never had a dog . . .

File. Oh, I had a dog.

Sheriff (*defensively*) When did you have a dog?

File. When I was a kid.

Sheriff (*testing for the truth of it*) What kind of dog was it?

File. Mongrel. Just a kid's kind.

Sheriff. What'd you call him?

File. Dog.

Sheriff. No, I mean what was his name?

File. Dog.

Sheriff (*rising, exasperated*) Didn't you have no name for him?

File. Dog—that was his name—Dog.

Sheriff (*moving to the desk*) That ain't no fittin' name for a dog.

File. I don't see why not.

Sheriff (*shocked*) You don't see why not?

File. Nope. He always came when I called him.

Sheriff (*almost apoplectic*) Hell, man, you couldn't of liked him much if you didn't even give him a name.

File. Oh, I liked him a lot, Sheriff. Gave him everything he wanted. Took good care of him, too—better than he took care of himself.

Sheriff. Why? What happened to him?

File. Dumb little mutt ran under a buckboard.

Sheriff (*moving to L of File*) Well, hell—you figure everythin's gonna run away—or get run over?

File (*with a smile*) Oh, I dunno—I just don't want a dog, Sheriff. Not that I ain't obliged.

Sheriff. Stubborn as a mule. (*He puts on his hat*) Well, I guess I'll have a look around—see what's doin'. (*He moves to the exit*)

File. Yeah—sleeps on your feet, does he?

B

SHERIFF (*laughing*) Right on my feet. Right on my big old stinkin' feet. See you later, File.

(*The* SHERIFF *exits. When he has gone,* FILE *discovers a rip in his shirt. He takes a cigar box from his desk, opens it and extracts a needle and thread. He has just begun to mend the tear when he hears the voices of the* CURRY MEN. *Lest they catch him in the un-mannish act of sewing, he replaces the cigar box in the desk, and forgetting the needle, lets it dangle from his shirt.*

NOAH, JIM *and* H.C. *enter. They are embarrassed about their errand, and, although they have plotted a plan of action, they are nervous about its outcome.* NOAH *is sullenly against this whole manœuvre*)

FILE. Hey, H.C. Hey, boys.

H.C. ⎫
NOAH ⎬ (*together; ad lib.*) Hey, File.
JIM ⎭

FILE. Ridin' over, you boys see any sign of rain?

NOAH. Not a spit.

FILE (*with a trace of a smile, but not unkindly*) What's it like in Sweetriver?

NOAH (*tensing a little*) How'd we know? We ain't been to Sweetriver.

FILE. Sheriff says that Lizzie's been to Sweetriver.

H.C. Yeah.

FILE. What's it like?

NOAH. Dry.

FILE. How'd Lizzie like it in Sweetriver?

NOAH (*sensing that their legs are being pulled*) Fine—she liked it fine.

JIM (*readying for a fight*) Yeah—she liked it fine. Three barn dances, a rodeo, a Summer fair and larkin' all over the place. (*He laughs loudly*)

(NOAH *squirms as he realizes that* FILE *sees through them.* H.C. *feels queasy*)

H.C. (*jumping in*) How's your poker, File?

FILE. My what?

H.C. Poker.

FILE. Oh, I don't like poker much.

JIM. You don't! Don't you like "Spit in the Ocean"?

FILE. Not much.

H.C. We figured to ask you to play some cards.

FILE. I gave cards up a long time ago, H.C.

JIM (*stymied*) You did, huh?

FILE. Mm-hm.

(*There is a silent impasse.* JIM *suddenly sees the needle hanging from File's shirt*)

JIM. File, what's that hangin' down from your shirt?
FILE (*a little self-consciously*) Kinda looks like a needle.
H.C. It sure does.
JIM. What's the matter—your shirt tore?
FILE. Looks like it.
JIM. Fix it yourself, do you?
FILE. Sure do.
JIM (*clucking in sympathy*) Tch-tch-tch-tch-tch-tch.
FILE (*suppressing a smile*) Oh, I wouldn't say that, Jim. I been fixin' my own shirts ever since I became a widower back in Pedleyville.
JIM. Lizzie fixes all my shirts.
FILE. Well, it sure is nice to have a sister.
JIM (*significantly*) Or somethin'.

(*There is a silent impasse*)

FILE. Did—uh—did Lizzie come back from Sweetriver by herself?
NOAH (*tensing*) Sure! She went by herself, didn't she?
FILE (*with a dry smile*) That don't mean nothin'. I rode down to Leverstown to buy myself a mare. I went by myself but I came back with a mare.
JIM (*getting the point; starting to lose his temper*) Well, she didn't go to buy nothin'. Get it, File—nothin'.
FILE (*evenly*) Don't get ornery, Jim. I just asked a friendly question.
NOAH (*to Jim; with hidden warning*) Sure! Just a friendly question—don't get ornery.
H.C. (*baiting the trap for File*) I always say to Jim—the reason you ain't got no real friends is 'cause you're ornery. You just don't know how to make friends.
JIM (*hurt and angry*) Sure I do—sure I do.
H.C. No, you don't. (*Meaningfully*) Do you ever ask a fella out to have a drink? No! Do you ever say to a fella, "Come on home and have some supper"?
JIM (*suddenly remembering the objective; not sure how to spring the trap*) I guess you're right. I'm sorry, File. Didn't mean to get ornery. Come on out and have a drink.
NOAH (*reflexively*) Supper.
JIM (*realizing his error; quickly*) Yeah—come on home and have some supper.
FILE (*aware of the trap*) Guess I'll say no to supper, boys. (*With a flash of mischief*) But I'll be glad to go out and have a drink with you.
NOAH. We don't have time for a drink. But we been figurin' to ask you to supper one of these days.
FILE. Be glad to come—one of these days.
H.C. How about tonight?

FILE. Don't have the time tonight. Seems there's some kind of outlaw comin' this way. Fella named Tornado Johnson. Have to stick around.

NOAH. You don't know he'll come this way, do you?

FILE. They say he's Three Point bound.

H.C. But you don't know he'll be here tonight.

FILE. I don't know he won't be here tonight.

JIM. Why he might be down at Pedleyville or Peak's Junction. He might even be over at our place.

FILE (*quietly*) Well, I won't be over at your place, Jim.

JIM (*to H.C.; riled*) You said for me to be friendly. Well, I'm tryin' but he don't want to be friendly.

FILE (*evenly*) I want to be friendly, Jim—but I don't want to be married.

(*There is a flash of tense silence*)

JIM (*exploding*) Who says we're invitin' you over for Lizzie? You take that back.

FILE (*rising*) Won't take nothin' back, Jim.

JIM. Then take somethin' else. (*His fist flashes out*)

(FILE *is too quick for Jim. He parries the single blow and levels off one of his own. It connects squarely with Jim's eye and* JIM *goes down. The fight is over that quickly*)

NOAH (*to File; tensely*) If I didn't think he had it comin', I'd wipe you up good and clean.

FILE. He had it comin'.

(*There is a brief pause.* NOAH *is the most humiliated of all of them.* JIM *rises*)

NOAH (*to H.C. more than to File*) I guess we all did. (*To Jim*) Come on, turtlehead, let's go home.

(NOAH *exits quickly.*
JIM *follows him off.* H.C. *remains with File. There is a silence*)

FILE (*quietly*) I shouldn't of hit him, H.C.

H.C. Oh, that's all right. Only thing is—you know you lost that fight.

FILE. What?

H.C. Yeah. It wouldn't of hurt you to come to supper. It mighta done you some good.

FILE. We weren't talkin' about supper.

H.C. (*meeting the confrontation squarely*) That's right. We were talkin' about Lizzie. And she mighta done you some good, too.

FILE. I can mend my own shirts.

H.C. Seems to me you need a lot more mendin' than shirts. (*He moves towards the exit*)

FILE. Wait a minute, H.C.

(H.C. *stops and turns*)

You don't drop a word like that and just leave it.

H.C. All right—what'd you hit him for?

FILE. He threw a punch. I got angry.

H.C. Angry—why? We come around here and say we like you enough to have you in our family. Is that an insult?

FILE. I don't like people interferin'.

H.C. Interferin' with what?

FILE. I'm doin' all right—by myself.

H.C. You ain't doin' all right. A fella who won't make friends with a whole town that likes him and looks up to him—a fella who locks himself in—he ain't doing all right. And if he says he is, he's a liar.

FILE. Take it easy, H.C.

H.C. I said a liar and I mean it. You talk about yourself as bein' a widower. We all got respect for your feelin's—but you ain't a widower—and everybody in this town knows it.

FILE (*losing his temper*) I am a widower. My wife died six years ago—back in Pedleyville.

H.C. Your wife didn't die, File—she ran out on you. And you're a divorced man. But we'll all go on calling you a widower as long as you want us to. Hell, it don't hurt us none—but you . . . A fella who shuts himself up with that lie—he needs mendin'. (*He pauses*) Want to throw any more punches?

FILE *slowly turns from H.C.*

H.C. *exits.* FILE, *brooding, sits at the desk and resumes the mending of his shirt, but his mind is not on it: his thoughts are turned inward as—*

the LIGHTS *fade to* BLACK-OUT

The LIGHTS *come up on the living-room, leaving the office and tack-room in darkness.* LIZZIE *is just finishing the supper preparations. She works competently and quickly, bubbling with excitement. She gives a quick survey of the kitchen, everything is fine. Now she has to dress. She moves* C *and notices there are only four chairs around the table. She shoves two chairs apart, gets the chair from* L *of the window up* C *and pushes it against the table to make the fifth. The sight of five chairs instead of the customary four is exhilarating to her. Singing, she hurries towards the stairs.* NOAH *enters* R. *He is in low, disgruntled spirits, but seeing Lizzie he tries to smile.*

LIZZIE. You all back so soon? (*She chatters excitedly*) Now don't walk heavy because the lemon cake will fall. You told File six o'clock, I hope?

NOAH. Uh—we didn't tell him no exact time.

LIZZIE (*in a spate of words*) Now that's real smart. Suppose he comes at seven and all the cooking goes dry. I got the prettiest lemon cake in the oven—and a steak and kidney pie as big as that table. Oh, look at me—I better change my dress or I'll get caught looking a mess. (*She turns to the stairs*)

NOAH (*trying to detain Lizzie*) Lizzie . . .

(*The telephone rings*)

LIZZIE. Answer the telephone, will you, Noah? And don't let Jimmy near the table. He'll mess it up.

(LIZZIE *exits hurriedly up the stairs. The telephone rings again.* NOAH *crosses to the telephone and lifts the receiver*)

NOAH (*into the telephone*) Hello . . .

(JIM *enters* R. *He has an effulgent black eye*)

(*Annoyed at the instrument*) Hello—hello . . . No, this ain't Jim— it's Noah. Who's this? . . . (*To Jim. Darkly*) It's Snookie Maguire.

JIM. Hot dog! (*He catapults across the room and reaches for the receiver*)

(NOAH, *with one hand over the mouthpiece, withholds the receiver from Jim with his other hand*)

NOAH. What exactly do you mean—"Hot dog"?

JIM (*lamely*) Just—hot dog, Noah.

NOAH. What are you gonna say to her?

JIM. I don't know what she's gonna say to me.

NOAH (*handing the receiver to Jim*) Well, watch out. (*He crosses to* RC)

JIM (*into the telephone; cooing lovingly*) Hello—hello, Snookie . . . Oh, I'm fine—I'm just fine and dandy. How are you? . . . Fine' and dandy? . . . Well, I'm sure glad you're fine and dandy too . . .

NOAH (*muttering disgustedly*) Fine-and-dandy-my-big-foot!

JIM (*into the telephone; so sweetly*) I was gonna telephone you, Snookie, but you telephoned me, di'n't you? . . . Ain't that the prettiest coincidence . . .

NOAH (*nauseated*) Jimmy, for Pete sake!

JIM (*into the telephone*) What? . . . You mean it, Snookie? . . . You mean it? . . . Gee, I sure hope you mean it . . .

NOAH. What's all that you mean it about?

JIM (*to Noah; in raptures*) She says, "It's a hot night and the Essex is sayin', 'Chug-chug, where's little Jimmy?' "

NOAH. Well, you tell her, "Chug-chug, little Jimmy's gonna sit home on his little fat bottom."

JIM. Now, wait a minute, Noah . . .

NOAH. Don't say wait a minute. If you wanta get mixed up with poison, you go right ahead. But I wash my hands.

JIM (*into the telephone; unhappily*) Hello, Snookie . . . I just can't tonight . . . (*Confused*) Well, I don't *know* why, exactly. Anyway,

I can't talk now . . . Oh, Snookie—(*longingly*) are you still wearin' your little red hat? . . . (*Relieved*) That's fine, Snookie—you take care of that . . . Good-bye, Snookie. (*He replaces the receiver*)

NOAH. See that? You go out with her once and she starts chasin' you.

JIM. Well, I don't see what's wrong with that, Noah.

NOAH (*shocked*) You don't?

JIM. No. People want to get together—they oughta get together. It don't matter how, does it?

NOAH (*crossing to the dresser*) Now you ask yourself if it don't really matter. (*He takes a ledger from the cupboard*) Go on and ask yourself, Jimmy. (*He crosses and sits on the chest*)

JIM (*suddenly lost when he has to figure it out for himself*) Well, maybe it does. (*He crosses to the radio*) Holy mackerel, I sure wish I could figure things out. (*He switches on the radio*)

(*The radio screeches*)

If only I could get somethin' on this crystal set—somethin'. You think I could get Kansas City on this thing?

NOAH (*intent on his ledger*) Nope!

JIM. Yeah? Well, maybe I got it and I didn't know it. The other day I fiddled with the set and suddenly I hear a sound like the prettiest music. And I says to myself: "Sonofagun, I got Kansas City."

NOAH. Static—that's all—just static.

JIM (*switching off the radio*) I knew you'd say that, Noah. And I figured the answer to it. If it feels like Kansas City, it is Kansas City.

NOAH. Then why don't you make it feel like Africa?

JIM. On this little crystal set?

(H.C. *enters* R)

H.C. (*moving to Noah*) Where's Lizzie? Did you tell her?

NOAH. No—she ran upstairs to get dressed.

(LIZZIE *enters hurriedly down the stairs. She is all dressed up and in a flurry of anticipation*)

LIZZIE (*moving* C) Well, folks, how do I look?

H.C. (*crossing to* R *of Lizzie*) Beautiful!

JIM. Great—beautiful!

LIZZIE. You know, Pop—I really think I am—if you don't look too close. (*Exuberantly*) When do you suppose File will get here? I ought to know some time we can start eating.

H.C. (*crossing and sitting on the settee; quietly*) We can start any time you say.

LIZZIE. Any time? (*She looks quickly at H.C. and quickly gets the point. Then, pretending that life goes on unchanged, even trying to see some advantage in File's not coming, she rattles on with studied casualness*) Well, you better wash up—and we can have more room at the table, and—(*she goes to the table to remove the fifth chair, but cannot bring herself to do it*) File's not coming . . .

H.C. No.

(LIZZIE *moves to the door* R)

JIM (*quickly*) Not that he didn't want to come. He wanted to —a lot. (*He crosses towards the kitchen*)

LIZZIE. He did, huh?

JIM. Sure. Pop said: "Come to supper tonight, File." And when Pop said that . . . (*To H.C. Quickly*) Did you notice how his face kinda—well—it lighted up? Did you notice that?

H.C. (*lamely*) Yeah.

JIM. And then File said: "Sure—sure I'll come. Glad to come." And then suddenly he remembered.

LIZZIE (*not at all taken in; quietly*) What did he remember, Jimmy?

JIM (*crossing to Lizzie*) Well, he remembered there's some kind of outlaw runnin' round. And he better stick around and pay attention to his job. Business before pleasure. Yessir—File was real friendly.

LIZZIE. Friendly, huh? What happened to your eye? (*She pulls Jim* C)

JIM. It kinda swole up on me.

NOAH. File hit him.

LIZZIE. You mean you fought to get him to come here?

JIM. It was only a little fight, Lizzie.

LIZZIE (*trying to laugh*) Why didn't you make it a big one—a riot? Why didn't you all just pile on and slug him?

JIM (*sitting* L *of the table*) Lizzie, you're seein' this all wrong.

LIZZIE. I'm seeing it the way it happened. He said: "She might be a pretty good cook—and it might be a good supper—but she's plain. She's as plain as old shoes."

H.C. He didn't say anything like that.

JIM. He didn't say nothin' about shoes.

H.C. Lizzie—we made a mess out of it.

NOAH. If you'd a taken my advice there wouldn't of been a mess. I said don't go down and talk to File—nobody listened. I said don't send her to Sweetriver—nobody listened. Hell, I don't like to be right all the time. But for God's sake . . .

H.C. (*rising and moving up* C) Well, Noah, I'm stumped. If you were Lizzie's father, what would you do?

NOAH (*rising and moving to* R *of the table*) Who says we gotta do anything? We been pushin' her around—tryin' to marry her off. Why? What if she don't get married? Is that the end of everything? She's got a home. She's got a family—she's got bed and board and clothes on her back and plenty to eat.

LIZZIE (*moving to* L *of Jim*) That's right. From now on we listen to Noah.

H.C. No! Don't you dare listen to him.

NOAH (*sitting* R *of the table*) Why not? She's got everything she needs.

H.C. She ain't got what'll make her happy.

JIM. And she ain't gonna get it.

(*They all look at Jim in surprise*)

Because she's goin' at it all wrong.

LIZZIE. How, Jimmy? How am I going at it wrong?

JIM. Because you don't talk to a man the way you oughta. You talk too serious. And if there's anything scares hell out of a fella it's a serious-talkin' girl.

(LIZZIE *moves to the settee and sits on it*)

H.C. Well, that's the way Lizzie is—and she can't be anything else.

JIM. Yes, she can. She's as smart as any of them girls down at the Ladies' Social Club. She can go down to the Social on Wednesday nights—and she can giggle and flirt as good as any of them.

H.C. What do you want her to turn into—Lily Ann Beasley?

JIM. Lily Ann Beasley gets any man she goes for. Why, I saw her walk up to Phil Mackie one mornin'—and she wiggled her hips like a cocker spaniel and she said: "Phil Mackie, how many toes have you got?" And he said, "Well, naturally—I got ten." And she said, "Why, that's just the right number of toes for a big strong man to have." And pretty soon he was cooked. He started followin' her around—and she got him so nervous, he bust right out with the shingles.

LIZZIE. Well, if she wants Phil Mackie she can have him— shingles and all.

JIM. And how about that livestock fella from Chicago?

LIZZIE. Jimmy—can I treat a man the way she treated him? (*She imitates Lily Ann*) "My—a polka-dot tie. I just adore a man with a polka-dot tie. Those little round dots go right to my heart."

JIM. Yeah—and that poor fella—the blood rushed out of his face and I thought he'd keel right over in the horse trough.

LIZZIE (*rising and moving towards the kitchen*) I don't want a man to keel over. I want him to stand up straight—and I want to stand up straight to him. Without having to trick him. (*With a cry*) Isn't that possible with a man—isn't it possible?

NOAH. No, it ain't.

H.C. Yes, it is, Lizzie.

NOAH. No. For once in his life, Jim said somethin' sensible. (*He confronts Lizzie. Quietly*) If it's a man you want, you gotta get him the way a man gets got.

LIZZIE. If that's the way a man gets got, I don't want any of them.

H.C. Lizzie . . .

LIZZIE. No! To hell with File. To hell with all of them!

NOAH. Don't use that language.

LIZZIE. Hell—hell—hell! To hell with all of them! (*It is an outcry straight from the heart, rebellious but aching*)

(*The others can do nothing to help Lizzie. The door* R *suddenly swings open, screaming on its hinges, and whacking the wall like a pistol shot. They all turn towards the door, but all they can see is a vista of sky, no-one is there.*

BILL STARBUCK, *visible to the audience, is just outside the door* R. *He is a big man, lithe, agile, a loud braggart, but a gentle dreamer. He carries a short hickory stick. It is his weapon, his pointer, his magic wand, his pride of manhood*)

NOAH. Who opened that door?

JIM. Musta been the wind.

(STARBUCK *steps on to the threshold. He hears Jim's line about the wind*)

STARBUCK. Wind? Did you say wind? There's not a breath of wind anywhere in the world.

NOAH. Who are you?

STARBUCK. The name's Starbuck. Starbuck is the name. (*He espies Lizzie and his whole manner changes. He doffs his hat and his bow is part gallantry, part irony. He crosses to her*) Lady of the house —hello.

LIZZIE (*involuntarily*) Hello.

STARBUCK. That's a mighty nice dress—it oughta go to a party.

H.C. (*moving down* RC) What is it? What can we do for you?

STARBUCK. You're askin' the wrong question. The question is what can I do for you?

NOAH. I don't remember we called for anybody to do anything.

STARBUCK. You should have, mister—you sure should have. You need a lot of help. You're in a parcel of trouble. You lost twelve steers on the north range and sixty-two in the gully. The calves are starvin' and the heifers are down to their knees.

JIM (*rising, crossing and standing up* RC) You know a heckuva lot about our herd.

STARBUCK (*noticing Jim's black eye*) Man, that sure is a shiner. (*To H.C.*) Your ranch, mister?

NOAH. He owns it—I run it.

STARBUCK (*to Noah*) Well, I guess I'll talk to you. You got a look of business about you, mister. You got your feet apart—and you stand solid on the ground. That's the kind of a man I like to talk to. Well, what are you gonna do about them cattle?

NOAH. If you know we lost the cattle, you oughta know what killed them. Drought. Ever hear of it?

STARBUCK. Hear of it! That's all I hear. Wherever I go, there's drought ahead of me. But when I leave—behind me there's rain —rain.

LIZZIE (*moving above the settee*) I think this man's crazy.

STARBUCK (*crossing and standing down* L) Sure—that's what I am—crazy. I woke up this mornin'—I looked at the world and I said to myself: "The world's gone completely out of its mind. And the only thing that can set it straight is a first-class, A-number-one lunatic." Well, here I am, folks—crazy as a bedbug. Did I introduce myself? The name is Starbuck—Rainmaker.

H.C. (*doubtfully*) I've heard about rainmakers. (*He indicates the chair below the table*)

STARBUCK (*sitting below the table*) Thank you, mister.

NOAH. I read about a rainmaker . . .

STARBUCK. What'd you read, mister?

NOAH. I can't remember whether they locked him up or ran him out of town.

STARBUCK (*laughing good-naturedly*) Might be they strung him up on a sycamore tree.

NOAH. Look, fella, the idea is—we don't believe in rainmakers.

STARBUCK. What *do* you believe in, mister—dyin' cattle?

JIM. You really mean you can bring rain?

LIZZIE. He talks too fast—he can't bring anything.

JIM (*crossing and sitting on the hassock*) I asked him. (*To Starbuck*) Can you bring rain?

STARBUCK. It's been done, brother—it's been done.

JIM (*excitedly*) Where? How?

STARBUCK (*rising; with a flourish of his stick*) How? Sodium chloride. Pitch it up high—right up to the clouds. Electrify the cold front. Neutralize the warm front. Barometricize the tropopause. Magnetize occlusions in the sky. (*He crosses to the door* R)

LIZZIE. In other words—bunk!

(STARBUCK, *realizing he will have to contend with Lizzie and Noah, suddenly and shrewdly reverses his field and agrees with Lizzie*)

STARBUCK. Lady, you're right! You know why that sounds like bunk? Because it is bunk. Bunk and hokey-pokey. And I tell you, I'd be ashamed to use any of those methods.

JIM. What method do you use?

STARBUCK (*crossing to* LC) My method's like my name—it's all my own. You want to hear my deal?

LIZZIE. We're not interested.

NOAH. Not one bit.

H.C. (*moving* C) What is it?

NOAH. Pop, you're not listenin' to this man . . .

H.C. (*moving to* R *of Starbuck; quietly*) Any charge for listenin'?

STARBUCK. No charge—free.

H.C. (*crossing to the chest and sitting*) Go ahead. What's the deal?

STARBUCK (*moving* C) One hundred dollars in advance—and inside of twenty-four hours you'll have rain.

JIM (*in a dither*) You mean it? Real rain?

STARBUCK. Rain is rain, brother. It comes from the sky. It's a wetness known as water. *Aqua pura.* Mammals drink it, fish swim in it, little boys wade in it, and birds flap their wings and sing like sunrise. Water! (*He picks up the pitcher from the table and pours some water over his head*) I recommend it.

JIM (*rising and crossing to Noah; convinced*) Pay him the hundred, Noah.

LIZZIE (*moving up* LC) Noah, don't be a chump!

NOAH. Me? Don't worry—I won't.

JIM. We got the drought, Noah. It's rain, Lizzie—we need it.

LIZZIE. We won't get a drop of it—not from him.

H.C. (*quietly*) How would you do it, Starbuck?

STARBUCK. Now don't ask me no questions.

LIZZIE. Why? It's a fair question. How will you do it?

STARBUCK. What do you care how I do it, sister, as long as it's done? But I'll tell you how I'll do it. I'll lift this stick and take a long swipe at the sky and let down a shower of hailstones as big as canteloupes. I'll shout out some good old Nebraska cusswords and there's a lake where your corral used to be. Or I'll just sing a little tune, maybe, and it'll sound so pretty and sound so sad you'll weep and your old man will weep and the sky will get all misty-like and shed the prettiest tears you ever did see. How'll I do it? Girl, I'll just do it.

NOAH. Where'd you ever bring rain before?

LIZZIE. What town? What state?

STARBUCK. Sister, the last place I brought rain is now called Starbuck—they named it after me. Dry? I tell you, those people didn't have enough damp to blink their eyes. So I get out my big wheel and my rolling drum and my yella hat with the three little feathers in it. I look up at the sky and I say: "Cumulus," I say: "Cumulo-nimbus. Nimbulo-cumulus." And pretty soon— way up there—there's a teeny little cloud the size of a mare's tail—and then over there—there's another cloud lookin' like a white-washed chicken coop. And then I look up and all of a sudden there's a herd of white buffalo stampedin' across the sky. And then, sister-of-all-good-people, down comes the rain. (*He crosses to the door* R) Rain in buckets, rain in barrels, fillin' the low-lands, floodin' the gullies. And the land is as green as the valley of Adam. And when I rode out of there I looked behind me and I see the prettiest colours in the sky—green, blue, purple, gold—colours to make you cry. And me? I'm ridin' right through that rainbow. Well, how about it? Is it a deal? (*He crosses to* C)

H.C. Well . . .

LIZZIE (*seeing H.C.'s indecision*) Pop—no! He's a liar and a con man.

H.C. (*reluctantly*) Yep, that's what he is all right—a liar and a con man.

STARBUCK (*collecting his hat*) Hurts me to hear you say that, mister. Well, so long to you—so long for a sorry night. (*He crosses towards the door* R)

H.C. Wait a minute.

STARBUCK (*stopping and turning*) You said I was a con man.

H.C. (*moving to* L *of Starbuck*) You're a liar and a con man—but I didn't say I wouldn't take your deal.

LIZZIE. Pop . . .

H.C. (*to Lizzie; quietly*) I didn't say I would, neither.

NOAH. Pop, you ain't gonna throw away a hundred bucks! How do I write it in the books?

H.C. Write it as a gamble, Noah. I've lost more'n that in poker on a Saturday night.

LIZZIE (*moving to the settee and sitting*) You get an even chance in poker.

H.C. Lizzie, I knew an old fella once—and he had the asthma. He went to every doctor and still he coughed and still he wheezed. Then one day a liar and a con man come along and took the old man for fifty dollars and a gold-plated watch. But a funny thing —after that con man left, the old boy never coughed again until the day he was kicked in the head by a horse.

LIZZIE. That's a crazy reason.

STARBUCK. I'll give you better reasons, Lizzie-girl. (*He crosses to* LC) You gotta take my deal because once in your life you gotta take a chance on a con man. You gotta take my deal because there's dyin' calves that might pick up and live. Because a hundred bucks is only a hundred bucks—but rain in a dry season is a sight to behold. You gotta take my deal because it's gonna be a hot night—and the world goes crazy on a hot night—and maybe that's what a hot night is for.

H.C. (*moving* RC) Starbuck, you got you a deal.

STARBUCK (*with a sudden smile*) Tell you: I knew I had a deal the minute I walked into this house.

JIM. How'd you know that?

STARBUCK. I see four of you and five places set for supper. And I says to myself: "Starbuck, your name's written right on—(*he indicates the chair below the table*) that chair."

H.C. (*with a laugh*) Let's eat.

STARBUCK *tosses his hat on to the pegs, turns the chair below the table to face it, and is the first to sit.* LIZZIE *rises and moves towards the kitchen.* H.C. *and* JIM *move towards the table as—*

the CURTAIN *falls*

ACT II

Scene—*The living-room.*

When the Curtain *rises, the* Lights *come up on the living-room, leaving the office and tack-room in darkness. It is evening and the lamps are lit. Supper is over and* Lizzie, *having cleared the dishes, is collecting the tablecloth.* Noah *is standing* r *of the table, paying Starbuck his fee, counting out the money on to the table. H.C. is seated above the table, quietly watching.* Jim, *with keyed-up excitement, is seated on the settee.* Lizzie *is hostile to the whole situation.* Starbuck *is seated below the table.*

Noah (*fuming as he counts out the notes*) Seventy—eighty—eighty-five . . . I'm against this, Pop.

H.C. (*quietly*) Keep countin', Noah.

Noah. Ninety—ninety-five—one hundred. There's your hundred bucks.

Starbuck (*picking up the notes*) Thank you, Noah.

(Lizzie *crosses to the porch, shakes out the tablecloth, then folds it and crosses to the dresser*)

Noah. Don't thank me—thank him. (*He crosses to the dresser, collects his ledger, pen and ink and returns to the table*) I'm writin' that down in my book. (*He sits* r *of the table*) One hundred dollars—thrown away. (*He opens the ledger and writes in it*)

Starbuck (*rising and crossing to the door* r) No—don't write that, Noah. Write it like this. Say: "On August the twenty-seventh, a man come stompin' through our door-way. We bid him time of night, we fed him a supper fit for a king and we gave him one hundred honest notes on the fair government of the United States of America. And in return for that hospitality he did us one small favour—he brought rain." (*With a smile*) You got that? Write it.

Noah. I don't see no rain yet.

Starbuck (*crossing to* c) I still got twenty-three hours to bring it.

(Lizzie *puts the cloth in the dresser drawer*)

Noah. Well, you better get busy.

Jim (*eagerly*) Yeah, Starbuck, you better knuckle down.

(Starbuck *moves to the chair* c *and is about to sit, but* Lizzie *takes it from under him and puts it* l *of the window up* c)

Starbuck. Now, let's not get nervous. Rain, my friends, rain comes to the man that ain't nervous. (*He crosses and sits beside Jim on the settee. Getting down to work*) Now—what kind of rain would you like?

JIM. You mean we can choose our kind?

(LIZZIE *collects a book from the dresser, crosses to the chest, sits and reads*)

STARBUCK. Sure you can choose your kind. And, brother, there's all kinds. There's mizzle and there's drizzle—but you wouldn't want that. I generally give that away as a free sample. There's trickle and there's sprinkle. But that's for the little flower gardens of little pink old ladies. There's April showers that I can bring in April—but I can sometimes bring 'em in May. There's rain with thunder and rain with hail. There's flash floods—and storms that roll down the shoulder of the mountain. But the biggest of all—that's deluge. (*Modestly*) But don't ask me for deluge—that takes a bit of doin'.

JIM. What kind do we get for a hundred bucks?

STARBUCK. You choose it and I'll bring it.

LIZZIE. He brags so loud he gives me a pain in the neck.

STARBUCK (*rising and moving* LC) Look, folks, if you all act like she does, it's gonna make it mighty tough for me to do my job. Because when there's suspicion around, it's a d-r-y season.

(JIM *rises and moves to* L *of Starbuck*)

LIZZIE (*rising and crossing to the settee*) I don't doubt it. (*She sits*)

STARBUCK. Well, she don't believe in me. How about the rest of you?

NOAH. What do you mean—believe in you? We certainly don't.

STARBUCK. Then I changed my mind. I don't want your money—take it back. (*In a temper, he slams the money on the table*)

(*The others are stunned*)

H.C. Noah—please. We made a bargain—it's settled. Now be a good sport.

NOAH (*exasperated*) Good sport! What's he expect me to say?

STARBUCK. I'll explain it to you, Noah. Makin' rain—it takes a lot of confidence. And if you have doubts about me—I get doubts about myself.

NOAH. Oh, I see. If you don't bring rain, you're gonna blame it on us. We didn't have confidence. Well, we don't.

LIZZIE. You can steal our money—but that's all you can steal.

STARBUCK (*in a temper*) That's not the right attitude.

JIM (*manfully*) I got the right attitude—take back your dough.

STARBUCK. No! What if I need some help?

JIM. I'll help you—so will Pop.

STARBUCK. But not him.

NOAH (*to Starbuck*) What kind of help?

STARBUCK (*moving above the settee*) Nothin' you can't do. (*To Lizzie*) How about you, lady? Any confidence?

LIZZIE. No confidence.

JIM (*picking up the notes and moving to R of Starbuck*) We don't need her. Starbuck—here's your dough.

(STARBUCK *takes the notes and puts them in his pocket*)

Now—what's the first step?

STARBUCK (*circling the settee and moving C*) Well, what I'm gonna ask you to do—it ain't gonna make sense. But what's sensible about a flood or a hurricane?

JIM. Nothin'.

STARBUCK. Right! Now—what I want you to do—(*he hurries to the window up R and points out*) you see that little old wagon of mine? On that wagon I got me a big brass drum. Somebody's gotta beat that drum.

NOAH. Beat it? What for?

(JIM *crosses to the chest*)

STARBUCK. Don't ask questions.

JIM (*catching on to the rules of the game*) And don't get sensible.

STARBUCK. That's right, Jimmy. Who's gonna beat that drum?

JIM (*the stalwart*) Me—I'll beat it.

STARBUCK. Jim—you're gonna be my first lieutenant. Now, you go on out there and every time you get the feelin' for it, you beat that drum—three times—boom—boom—boom—low, like thunder—got it?

JIM. Got it! Every time I get the feelin'?

STARBUCK. That's it.

JIM (*eagerly*) When do I start?

STARBUCK. Mister, you've started.

(JIM *exits quickly R*)

(*He moves to L of the table and sits*) Mister H.C., I want you to pay close attention. In that wagon I got a bucket of white paint. Now it ain't ordinary white paint—it's special. It's electro-magnetized, oxygenated, dechromated white. Now, I want you to go out there and paint a great big white arrow pointin' away from the house. That's so the house don't get struck by lightnin'.

H.C. (*rising and moving to the door R; with a wry smile*) That sounds reasonable.

STARBUCK (*pretending to talk to himself, but with his eye on Noah*) Now—it's too bad you ain't got a mule on the place.

NOAH (*muttering*) We got a mule.

STARBUCK. You have? That's great—that's just dandy. Noah, get a length of strong rope and go out there and tie that mule's hind legs together.

NOAH. What! Tie the hind legs of a mule? What the hell for?

STARBUCK (*hurt*) Please—now, please—you gotta do like I ask you.

NOAH. I ain't gonna do it.

H.C. (*moving to Noah*) Come on, Noah.

(NOAH *rises.* H.C. *leads him to the door* R)

NOAH. I'll be damned—tie the hind legs of a mule.

(NOAH, *in a huff, exits hurriedly* R. H.C. *starts to follow him when Lizzie's voice stops him*)

LIZZIE (*rising and moving* C) Pop—wait. (*Livid with rage*) Pop—I'm ashamed of you. I've been sitting here—keeping my mouth shut—wondering how far you'd let this man go in making a fool of you.

H.C. (*quietly*) He can't make me any more fool than I make out of myself.

LIZZIE. Where's your commonsense? Hang on to a little of it.

H.C. You mean go along with this fella halfway, huh? Well, I can't do that. I gotta take a chance on him—the whole chance—without fear of gettin' hurt or gettin' cheated or gettin' laughed at—as far as he'll take me. (*He turns to Starbuck, and confronts him levelly*) A white arrow, did you say?

(*There is a short pause, then* STARBUCK, *meeting* H.C.'s *glance, responds seriously, even respectfully*)

STARBUCK. A white arrow, H.C.

H.C. (*moving to the door* R) I'll paint it.

STARBUCK (*rising and moving* RC; *with the faintest touch of desperation*) Dammit, mister, you're gonna get your money's worth if it's the last thing I do.

H.C. (*with a quiet smile; gently*) Don't get nervous, boy.

STARBUCK. I ain't—not a bit of it.

H.C. That's fine. Confidence!

(H.C. *exits* R. *From outdoors, we hear the first deep pompous sound of the bass drum, boom, boom, boom*)

STARBUCK (*calling to Jim*) Attaboy, Jim—you beat that drum. Make it rumble.

JIM (*off; calling; in the spirit of things*) Make it rumbllll.

(*The sound of the drum is heard off.* LIZZIE, *fuming with anger, whirls on Starbuck*)

LIZZIE. Well! I'll bet you feel real proud of yourself.

STARBUCK (*smiling evenly*) Kinda proud, sure.

LIZZIE (*raging*) You're not satisfied to steal our money. You have to make a jackass out of us. Why'd you send them out on those fool errands? Why? What for?

STARBUCK. Maybe I thought it was necessary.

C

Lizzie (*sitting on the settee*) You know good and well it wasn't necessary. (*She kicks Starbuck's stick from the hassock*) You know it.

Starbuck. Maybe I sent them out so's I could talk to you alone.

Lizzie (*her rage mounting*) Then why didn't you just say it straight out: "Lizzie, I want to talk to you—alone—man to man."

Starbuck (*quietly*) Man to man, Lizzie?

Lizzie (*bitingly*) Excuse me—I made a mistake—you're not a man. (*She fusses with the buttons on her dress*)

(Starbuck *tenses, then controls his anger*)

Starbuck. Lizzie, can I ask you a little question?

Lizzie. No.

Starbuck. I'll ask it, anyway. Why are you fussin' at the buttons of your dress?

Lizzie. Fussing at the . . .? I'm not. (*She stops fussing*)

Starbuck (*evenly and gently*) Let 'em alone. They're all buttoned up fine. (*He circles to* L *of Lizzie*) As tight as they'll ever get. And it's a nice dress, too. Brand new, ain't it? You expectin' somebody?

Lizzie. None of your business.

Starbuck. A woman gets all decked out—she must be expectin' her beau. Where is he? It's gettin' kinda late.

Lizzie (*rising; breaking out*) I'm not expecting anybody. (*She moves* c)

Starbuck (*quietly*) Oh, I see. You were—but now you ain't. Stand you up?

Lizzie. Mr Starbuck—you've got more gall . . . (*She crosses towards the stairs*)

Starbuck (*grabbing Lizzie's arm*) Wait a minute.

Lizzie. Let go of me.

Starbuck (*tensely*) The question I really wanted to ask you before—it didn't have nothin' to do with buttons. It's this: the minute I walked into your house—you didn't like me. Why?

Lizzie. I said let go.

Starbuck (*releasing her*) You didn't like me—why? Why'd you go up on your hind legs like a frightened mare?

Lizzie. I wasn't frightened, Mr Starbuck. You paraded yourself in here—and you took over everything. I don't like to be taken by a con man.

Starbuck (*lashing out*) Wait a minute! I'm sick and tired of this. I'm tired of you queerin' my work, callin' me out of my name.

Lizzie. I called you what you are—a big-mouthed liar and a fake.

Starbuck (*with mounting intensity*) How do you know I'm a liar? How do you know I'm a fake? Maybe I can bring rain. Maybe when I was born God whispered a special word in my ear. Maybe He said, "Bill Starbuck, you ain't gonna have much in this world. You ain't gonna have no wife and no kids—no green little house to come home to. But Bill Starbuck—wherever you go—you'll bring rain." Maybe that's my one and only blessing.

LIZZIE (*moving to* L *of the settee*) There's no such blessing in the world.

STARBUCK (*moving* C) I seen even better blessings, Lizzie—girl. I got a brother who's a doctor. You don't have to tell him where you ache or where you pain. He just comes in and lays his hand on your heart and pretty soon you're breathin' sweet again. And I got another brother who can sing—and when he's singin', that song is there—and never leaves you. (*With an outcry*) I used to think—why ain't I blessed like Fred or Arny? Why am I just a nothin' man, with nothin' special to my name? And then one Summer comes the drought—and Fred can't heal it away and Arny can't sing it away. But me—I go down to the hollow and I look up and I say: "Rain! Dammit—please—bring rain." And the rain came. And I knew—I knew I was one of the family.

(LIZZIE *sits on the settee, at the left end*)

(*Suddenly quiet. Angry with himself*) That's a story. You don't have to believe it if you don't want to. (*He sits* R *of Lizzie on the settee*)

(*There is a pause.* LIZZIE *is affected by the story, but she will not let herself be. She pulls herself together with some effort*)

LIZZIE. I don't believe it.

STARBUCK. You're like Noah. You don't believe in anything.

LIZZIE. That's not true.

STARBUCK. Yes, it is. You're scared to believe in anything. You put the fancy dress on—and the beau don't come. So you're scared that nothin'll ever come. You got no faith.

LIZZIE (*crying out*) I've got as much as anyone.

STARBUCK. You don't even know what faith is. And I'm gonna tell you. It's believin' you see white when your eyes tell you black. It's knowin'—with your heart.

LIZZIE. And I know you're a fake.

STARBUCK (*in sudden commiseration*) Lizzie, I'm sad about you. You don't believe in nothin'—not even in yourself. You don't even believe you're a woman. And if you don't—you're not.

(STARBUCK *rises abruptly, crosses and exits* R. LIZZIE *rises and stands there, still hearing his words. She is deeply perturbed by them The heat seems unbearable. The sound of the drum is heard off*)

LIZZIE (*upset; weakly*) Jimmy—please. Please—quit that.

JIM *does not hear and the sound of the drum continues.*
LIZZIE *rushes up the stairs as—*

the LIGHTS *fade to* BLACK-OUT

The LIGHTS *come up on File's office* R, *leaving the living-room and tackroom in darkness. The office is dimly illuminated by the goose-neck lamp on the desk and by the brilliant moonlight streaming through the window.* FILE *is lying on the couch staring unseeingly up at the ceiling. After a few moments he rises and stretches. He is unhappy and uncomfortable. He picks up a piece of cardboard from the desk, fans himself once or twice, then throws the cardboard down. The* SHERIFF *enters.*

FILE. Anything doin'?

SHERIFF. Not a thing—so I ran home for a while. Any calls?

FILE (*looking at a paper on the desk*) Peak's Junction called and said that Tornado Johnson fella was seen ridin' our way. Old Lady Keeley called and said she heard thunder.

SHERIFF. How can she? She's deaf as a post.

FILE. I thought I heard it, too. But it was too regular.

(*The sound of the drum is heard off in the distance*)

SHERIFF. There it is. Sure ain't thunder.

FILE. Lots of electricity in the air. My hair's full of it.

(*There is a long pause. The sound of the drum is heard off in the distance*)

SHERIFF. Mine, too. (*He removes his hat, sits on the stool and looks closely at File*) Phil Mackie says the Curry boys came by.

FILE. Oh, yes—I forgot.

SHERIFF. Anything important?

FILE. No.

SHERIFF (*rising*) Phil says he saw Jim Curry come out of here wearin' a black eye.

FILE. He did, huh?

SHERIFF. Yeah—and he wasn't wearin' it when he came in. What happened?

FILE (*with a flare of temper*) Tell Phil Mackie to mind his own damn business.

(*The sound of the drum is heard off in the distance*)

SHERIFF (*after a hurt pause; surprised*) And me to mind mine?

FILE. I'm sorry, Sheriff. (*He pauses moodily for a moment*) Sheriff —I been thinkin'—I changed my mind.

SHERIFF. About what?

FILE. That dog you were talkin' about.

SHERIFF. You did, huh?

FILE. Yes. If the offer still holds, I'd sure like to have him.

SHERIFF (*embarrassed*) Well, I'll tell you, File—you said you didn't want him. And little Bobby Easterfield come over—and my wife gave him away. I'm sorry, File.

FILE. Forget it.

SHERIFF. What made you change your mind about the dog, File?

File (*evasively*) Oh, I don't know.

Sheriff. Didn't have anything to do with the Currys, did it?

File. Now what the hell would my wantin' a dog have to do with the Currys, for God's sake?

Sheriff. Well—didn't it?

File (*after an instant*) All right—it did.

Sheriff. File, why don't you stop teasin' yourself? If you want to get yourself out of this stew—why don't you do it? Why don't you go over and see the Curry girl?

File. No! I ain't gonna be a dunce with a woman—not any more.

Sheriff. Because you were a dunce with one of them—do you have to be a dunce with all of them?

File. I don't want to go over and see her—and just stand there like a stick.

Sheriff. Don't stand. Sit! Talk!

File. I make up conversations—and they all stay in my head.

Sheriff. Well—flush 'em out.

(*The sound of the drum is heard off in the distance*)

File (*suddenly making up his mind*) Mind if I take an hour off?

Sheriff. Take two hours—take the whole night.

File. No—an hour's all I can stand.

File *exits. The* Sheriff's *eyes follow him with a pleased glance as—*

the Lights *fade to* Black-Out

The Lights *come up on the living-room, leaving the office and tack-room in darkness. The living-room is momentarily unoccupied. The sound of the drum is heard off.* H.C. *enters* r. *He carries a whitewash brush and a pail of white paint. His face is daubed with whitewash, as are his clothes. Bent nearly double from having been painting the arrow, he absent-mindedly puts the pail on the floor. He abruptly realizes that the paint bucket will leave a mark, snatches it up and puts it out on the porch. The sound of the drum is heard off. He looks at the mark on the floor, scurries guiltily into the kitchen, grabs a towel and rushes back to clean up the mess. About to apply the spotless towel to the floor he realizes one does not get paint on a clean towel. He tosses the towel into the kitchen, goes to the porch, collects a bundle of rag, kneels and wipes up the paint.* Noah, *unheard by* H.C., *enters* r. *He has had discourteous treatment by the recalcitrant mule and is limping. He stops at the sight of H.C. and watches him for a few moments.*

Noah (*standing in the doorway*) He said paint the ground, not the floor.

H.C. (*startled*) I ain't paintin' the floor—I'm cleanin' it. (*He rises*)

Noah (*getting a good look at H.C.*)   Your face is all over white-wash.

H.C. Yep—I reckon it is.

Noah. So's your shirt.

H.C. Yep.

Noah. To look at you, you'd think you never painted nothin' in your life.

H.C. (*sheepishly*) I didn't see the cactus.

Noah. What cactus?

H.C. (*annoyed*) I was paintin' backward and suddenly there was that damn cactus—and I bumped—and the paint slopped all over everything.

(Noah *crosses to the table*)

(*He notices Noah is limping*) What you limpin' about?

Noah. I'm not limpin'. (*He sits* R *of the table and works at his ledger*)

H.C. Mule kick you? (*He puts the rag out on the porch*)

(Noah *grunts*)

Bad?

Noah (*annoyed*) Bad or good, a mule's kick is a mule's kick.

(*The sound of the drum is heard off, louder than ever*)

(*He rises, goes to the window and calls cholerically*) Jim-my, for Pete sake—come in here and quit beatin' that drum. (*He resumes his seat at the table*)

(*The sound of the drum ceases*)

H.C. (*smiling*) I think he enjoys it.

Noah. Sure. He's got the easiest job of all of us.

H.C. (*crossing to* L *of the table and sitting*) Well, he's the lieutenant.

(Jim *enters* R. *He carries the biggest bass drum in the world. He just stands there in the doorway, grinning.* H.C. *and* Noah *stare at him. He beats the drum once, with a flourish, just for the hell of it*)

Noah. Jimmy, you quit that.

Jim (*putting the drum by the chest*) He said for me to beat it every time I get the feelin'.

H.C. (*tolerantly*) Well, Jimmy, if you can try to resist the feelin' we'll all appreciate it.

Jim. Holy mackerel, Pop, your face is all over whitewash.

H.C. (*feigning surprise*) It is, is it?

Jim. Yeah—so's your shirt.

H.C. Well, whattaya know?

Jim. Whyn't you wash up? You look foolish.

H.C. You don't look so bright yourself, totin' that drum.

Jim. What am I gonna do with it?

Noah (*rising; exasperated*) For the love of Mike, don't be so dumb. (*He collects his ledger and writing materials, crosses and puts them on the dresser*)

Jim (*hurt and angry*) Don't call me that, Noah.

(*There is a silence.* Noah *takes a set of draughts and board from the dresser cupboard, and puts them on the table*)

H.C. I didn't notice—anybody see a cloud?

Noah (*sitting* R *of the table*) Not a wisp of a one. And don't you expect it.

Jim. I wouldn't be so sure about that, Noah.

Noah. You wouldn't—I would.

Jim. I think he is gonna bring rain. Because I been lookin' in his wagon. Boy, he's got all kinds of wheels and flags and a bugle and firecrackers . . .

Noah. And all the kinds of stuff that a con man would have—but nothin' that got anything to do with rain.

Jim. You're wrong, Noah. (*He opens the chest and takes out a quilt*)

H.C. What are you doin' in Lizzie's linen chest?

Jim (*putting the quilt on top of the chest*) He asked me could he spend the night in the tack-room and I said yes. So I figured I'd get him somethin' to sleep on.

Noah. You're sure stretchin' yourself to make him cosy, ain't you?

Jim (*moving above the table*) Why not? I like him. (*He helps himself to some grapes from the bowl on the table*)

H.C. Funny—me, too.

Noah (*disgustedly*) He's certainly pullin' the wool over your eyes.

Jim. I'm out there with the drum—waitin' for the feelin' to come—and he comes over and we had a great talk, the two of us.

Noah. What'd he try to sell you *this* time?

Jim (*leaning over H.C.; in fervent defence of Starbuck*) Nothin'—he didn't try to sell me nothin'. He just come over—and I'm lookin' up at the sky—and he says: "What are you thinkin' about, Jim?" Real serious—like he give a damn.

H.C. And what'd you tell him?

Jim (*importantly*) I said: "Not much."

H.C. Well, that's a good start to a conversation.

Jim (*crossing down* L) And then before I know it, I'm tellin' him all about myself. And I'm tellin' him about Lizzie and about how Noah snores at night. And I even told him about Snookie.

Noah. Yeah?

Jim. Yeah! I says to him: "What do you think of a girl that wears loud clothes and puts lip rouge on her mouth and always goes around in a little red hat? Is she fast?" And you know what he said? (*Triumphantly*) He said: "Never judge a heifer by the flick of her tail."

H.C. (*suppressing a smile*) Sounds like sensible advice.

JIM. I think so. And then he says: "What do you think of the world?" And I say to him: "It's gonna get all swole up and bust right in our faces." And you know what he told me? (*This, to him, is the most wonderful part*) He said: "It's happened before—and it can happen again." (*He crosses to* RC)

NOAH. There! I told you he'd sell you a bill of goods.

JIM (*moving to the door* R; *angrily*) Noah, I understand that crack. You mean he was tryin' to make me feel smart—and I ain't.

NOAH. Oh, shut up.

JIM. No, I won't shut up.

NOAH. What the hell's got into you?

JIM (*moving above the table and sitting*) I just thought of somethin', Noah. You know the only time I feel real dumb?

NOAH. When?

JIM. When I'm talkin' to you. Now, why the hell is that, Noah?

(LIZZIE *enters down the stairs*)

H.C. Lizzie—I thought you went to bed.

LIZZIE. It's roasting up there.

H.C. It's too bad we don't have one of those electric fans.

LIZZIE. It's not only the heat. Jimmy and his drum. (*She crosses to the door* R)

(*The telephone rings.* NOAH *rises, crosses to the telephone and lifts the receiver.*

STARBUCK *appears outside the window up* C)

NOAH (*into the telephone*) Hello . . . Who? . . . No—he's not here. (*He summarily replaces the receiver*)

JIM. Who was that?

NOAH. Who else would have all that gall?

JIM (*rising*) Snookie! Noah, that call was for me.

NOAH. Well?

JIM (*angrily*) Why'd you hang up on her?

NOAH. Save you the trouble.

JIM (*crossing to Noah*) If she calls me on the phone, you don't have to tell her I ain't here. I can do it myself.

NOAH. How can you yourself tell her you ain't here? Talk sense.

JIM. Maybe it don't make sense but you damn well know what I mean.

NOAH (*incensed*) Listen, Jimmy. If you want to get yourself in hot water—all you have to do is lift that phone and call her right back.

STARBUCK (*outside the window; with studied casualness*)   He's right, Jimmy. That's all you have to do.

NOAH. Stay out of this.

STARBUCK. I'm just agreeing with you, Noah. (*To Jim*) You can call her right back.

(*There is a moment of painful indecision on* JIM's *part. He looks at Starbuck and at* NOAH, *who is standing squarely in front of the telephone*)

(*With quiet, urgent encouragement*) Go on, kid.

JIM (*looking at Noah; weakening*)   I—I don't have her telephone number.

STARBUCK. All you have to do is call the operator.

JIM (*miserably; more plea than anger*)   Let me alone, Starbuck.

STARBUCK. Go on.

(JIM *turns away*)

(*He turns to H.C.*) H.C., a word from you might be a lot of help.

H.C. (*quietly*)   He'll work it out, Starbuck.

(STARBUCK, *seeing that H.C. will not interfere, moves away from the window and appears outside the door* R)

STARBUCK. Lizzie. Tell Jimmy to make the call.

LIZZIE (*with difficulty*)   Starbuck, we'll all thank you not to interfere in our family.

STARBUCK (*squelched*)   Sorry—guess I'm a damn fool.

(STARBUCK *turns quickly on his heel and exits. There is a heavy silence in the room.* NOAH *crosses to* R. LIZZIE *notices the quilt on the chest*)

LIZZIE. What are these things doing here?

H.C. For Starbuck. Jimmy was going to take them out to the tack-room—if it's all right.

LIZZIE (*picking up the quilt and crossing to Jim*)   It's all right. Go on, Jimmy.

JIM. I don't want to now.

(JIM, *deeply upset, ashamed to face Starbuck, and ashamed to stay with the others, exits hurriedly up the stairs*)

LIZZIE (*quietly*)   You shouldn't have done that, Noah. (*She puts the quilt on the newel post, moves to the settee and sits*)

NOAH (*guiltily and unhappily*)   Somebody's gotta do it. (*He sits on the chest*)

LIZZIE. I think you liked doing it.

NOAH. No, I didn't. (*In a hurt outburst*) For Pete's sake—somebody take this family off my hands. I don't want to run it.

H.C. (*rising and moving up* RC)   You don't have to run the family, Noah—only the ranch.

NOAH. They're both tied up together. And if you don't like the way I do things . . .

H.C. (*interrupting*) That ain't so, Noah. There's some things you do real good.

NOAH (*in a pained outburst*) Then why don't you give me a little credit once in a while? I'm trying to keep this family goin'. I'm trying to keep it from breakin' its heart on one foolishness after another. And what do I get for it? Nothin' but black looks and complaints. (*Passionately*) Why—why?

H.C. (*crossing to* L *of the table*) Because you're tryin' to run the family the way you run the ranch.

NOAH. There's no other way.

H.C. Noah, when I was your age I had my nose pressed to the grindstone—just like you. Your mother used to say: "Let up, Harry—stop and catch your breath." Well, after she died I took her advice—on account of you three kids. And I turned around to enjoy my family. (*Quietly and urgently*) And I found out a good thing, Noah. If you let 'em live—people pay off better than cattle.

NOAH (*in low answer*) Don't be so proud of the way you let us live, Pop. (*He points to Lizzie*) Just look at her—and don't be so damn proud of yourself.

H.C. (*moving* RC; *angry and apprehensive*) What do you mean by that, Noah?

NOAH (*rising*) Never mind—you think about it.

(NOAH, *in a cold fury, exits* R. *There is a long silence. When* H.C. *speaks to Lizzie he does not look at her. There is heavy worry in his voice*)

H.C. What does he mean, Lizzie?

LIZZIE (*evasively*) I don't know. Don't pay any attention to him, Pop. (*She is itchy, restless. Her mood is mercurial, changing quickly between her yearning to find something new to do with herself, and her need to hide this yearning, perhaps by laughing at herself, by laughing at the world, by laughing at nothing at all*) I don't know whether I'm hungry or thirsty. You like something to eat?

H.C. No, thanks. Noah's hinting that I made some big mistakes with you, Lizzie. Did I?

LIZZIE (*with surface laughter and bravura*) Of course not. I'm perfect—everybody knows I'm perfect. A very nice girl—good housekeeper, bright mind, very honest. So damn honest it kills me. How about a sandwich?

H.C. (*puzzled by her mood; more definitely than before*) No, thanks.

LIZZIE. You gotta get a man like a man gets got. That's what Noah said. (*She laughs*) Now isn't that stupid? Why, it's not even good English.

H.C. (*soberly*) Don't think about that, Lizzie. (*He sits* R *of the table*)

LIZZIE (*protesting too much*) Think about it—why, I wouldn't give it a second thought. (*Abruptly*) Pop, do you know what that Starbuck man said to me?

H.C. (*quietly*) What, Lizzie?

LIZZIE. No—why repeat it? A man like that—if you go repeating what people like that have to say . . . (*Abruptly*) Why doesn't it rain? What we need is a flood—(*with sudden gaiety*) a great big flood—end of the world—ta-ta—goo'bye. (*Abruptly serious*) Pop, can a woman take lessons in being a woman?

H.C. You don't have to take lessons. You are one.

LIZZIE (*with an outcry*) Starbuck says I'm not.

H.C. (*after a split second of surprise*) If Starbuck don't see the woman in you, he's blind.

LIZZIE. Is File blind? Are they all blind? (*With deepening pain*) Pop, I'm sick and tired of me. I want to get out of me for a while—be somebody else.

H.C. Go down to the Social Club and be Lily Ann Beasley— is that what you want to be?

LIZZIE. Lily Ann Beasley knows how to get along.

H.C. Then you better call her on the telephone—ask her to let you join up.

LIZZIE (*defiantly*) I will—you see if I don't. And I'm going to buy myself a lot of new dresses—cut away down to here. And I'll get myself some bright lip rouge—and paint my mouth so it looks like I'm always whistling.

H.C. Fine—go ahead—look like a silly little jackass.

LIZZIE. It won't be *me* looking silly—it'll be somebody else. You've got to hide what you are. You can't be honest.

H.C. (*angrily*) You wouldn't know how to be anything else.

LIZZIE (*rising*) Oh, wouldn't I—wouldn't I? You think it's hard? It's easy. Watch me—it's easy—look at this. (*She crosses the room, swinging her hips voluptuously. When she speaks it is with a silly, giggling voice—imitating Lily Ann. She addresses H.C. as if he were Phil Mackie, the town oaf*)

(FILE, *unseen by the others, appears at the open door* R, *and witnesses most of Lizzie's improvisation*)

Why, Phil Mackie—how goodie-goo-lookin' you are. Such curly blonde hair, such pearly white teeth. C'n I count your teeth? One-two-three-four-nah-nah, mustn't bite. And all those muscle-ie muscles. Ooh, just hard as stone, that's what they are, hard as stone. Oh, dear, don't tickle—don't tickle—or little Lizzie's gonna roll right over and dee-I-die. (*She giggles uproariously, and as she continues this makeshow game, she carries herself into convulsions of laughter*)

(H.C., *seeing that Lizzie has unintentionally satirized the very thing she proposes to emulate, joins in her laughter*)

FILE. Good evening.

(*The laughter in the room ceases abruptly.* LIZZIE *stands* L, *stock still with mortification*)

H.C. (*rising and moving* C) Hello, File. Come in.

FILE. Kinda late. I hope I'm not disturbin' you.

H.C. No—no. We were just—well, I don't know what we were doin'—but come on in.

FILE (*coming into the room; quietly*) Hello, Lizzie.

LIZZIE. Hello, File.

FILE (*to H.C.; uncomfortably*) H.C., I got to thinkin' about the little fuss I had with Jimmy and—about his eye and—well—I wanted to apologize. I'm sorry.

H.C. (*moving to* L *of the table; with a hidden smile*) You said that this afternoon, File.

FILE. But I didn't say it to Jim.

H.C. That's true—you didn't. (*With a quick look at Lizzie*) He's upstairs—I'll send him down. (*He moves quickly up the stairs*)

(LIZZIE, *seeing it is* H.C.'s *plan to leave her alone with File, takes a quick step towards the stairs and, all innocence, calls up to Jim*)

LIZZIE (*calling*) Oh, Jim—Jimmy—can you come down for a minute?

H.C. (*with studied casualness*) That's all right, Lizzie—I was goin' up, anyway.

(H.C., *giving Lizzie no choice, exits up the stairs.* LIZZIE *and* FILE *are both aware of* H.C.'s *manœuvre. They are both painfully embarrassed and are unable to meet one another's glances*)

LIZZIE (*just to fill the silence*) How about a cup of coffee?

FILE. No, thank you—I already had my supper.

LIZZIE (*embarrassed at the mention of "supper"*) Yes—yes, of course.

FILE (*seeing her embarrassment*) I didn't mean to mention supper —sorry I said it.

LIZZIE (*moving up* LC) How about some nice cold lemonade?

FILE. No, thank you.

LIZZIE (*in agony; talking compulsively*) I make lemonade with limes. I guess if you make it with limes you can't really call it lemon-ade, can you?

FILE (*generously; to put her at ease*) You can if you want to. No law against it.

LIZZIE. But it's really lime-ade, isn't it?

FILE. Yep—that's what it is, all right.

LIZZIE (*taking his mannish tone*) That's what it is, all right.

(*There is an impasse; there is nothing more to talk about. There is a pause.*

Jim *enters down the stairs. He comes quickly down the steps and is all grins that File is visiting)*

Jim. You call me, Lizzie? Hey, File.

File. Hello, Jim. My, that's a bad eye. I came around to say I'm sorry.

(Jim, *delighted to have File here, is all forgiveness)*

Jim *(crossing to* l *of File; expansively)* Oh, don't think nothin' of it, File. Bygones is bygones.

File. Glad to hear you talk that way.

Jim. Sure—sure.

(*There is an awkward silence.* Jim's *grin fills the whole room. He looks from one to the other, not knowing what to say, not knowing how to get out)*

(*Abruptly*) Well, well! File's here, huh?

(*There is a silence*)

(*With a burst of enthusiasm*) Yessir—he certainly is.

(Jim *crosses to the drum and in sheer animal spirits, he gives one loud whack on it, then races out* r. *He leaves a vacuum behind him)*

File. Was that Jim's drum I been hearin'?

Lizzie. Yes.

File (*with a dry smile*) Didn't know he was musical.

Lizzie (*smiling at File's tiny little joke*) Uh—wouldn't you like to sit down—or somethin'?

File. No, thank you. (*He looks in the direction of Jim and H.C.*) I guess they both knew I was lying.

Lizzie. Lying? About what?

File. I didn't come around to apologize to Jim.

Lizzie. What did you come for, File?

File. To get something off my chest. (*His difficulties increasing*) This afternoon—your father—he—uh—(*diving in*) well, there's a wrong impression goin' on in the town—that I'm a widower. Well, I'm not.

Lizzie (*trying to ease things for him; quietly*) I know that, File. (*She moves to the settee and sits*)

File. I know you know it—but I gotta say it. (*Blurting it out*) I'm a divorced man.

Lizzie. You don't have to talk about it if you don't . . .

File (*moving* lc; *interrupting roughly*) Yes, I do. I came to tell the truth. I've been denyin' that I'm a divorced man—well, now I admit it. That's all I want to say—(*angrily*) and that squares me with everybody.

Lizzie (*soberly*) Does it?

File. Yes, it does. And from here on in—if I want to live alone—all by myself—it's nobody's business but my own. (*He has said what he thinks he came to say, and having said it, he turns on his heel and starts to beat a hasty retreat)*

Lizzie *(sharply)* Wait a minute.

(File *stops and turns*)

(She rises and moves c) You're dead wrong.

File. Wrong? How?

Lizzie *(hotly)* It's everybody's business.

File. How do you figure that, Lizzie?

Lizzie. Because you owe something to people.

File. I don't owe anything to anybody.

Lizzie. Yes, you do.

File. What?

Lizzie *(upset and inarticulate)* I don't know—friendship. If somebody holds out his hand toward you, you've got to reach—and take it.

File *(moving* RC) What do you mean—I've got to?

Lizzie *(in an outburst)* Got to. There are too many people alone. And if you're lucky enough for somebody to want you—for a friend—*(with a cry)* it's an obligation.

(There is a silence. File is deeply perturbed by what Lizzie has said; even more perturbed by her impassioned manner)

File. This—this ain't something the two of us can settle by just talkin' for a minute.

Lizzie *(tremulously)* No—it isn't.

File *(with a step towards her)* It'll take some time.

Lizzie. Yes. (*She moves to the settee and sits)*

(A spell has been woven between them. Suddenly it is broken. Noah enters R. *He is surprised to see File)*

Noah. Oh, you here, File?

File. Yeah, I guess I'm here.

Noah *(looking for an excuse to leave)* Uh—just comin' in for my feed book.

(Noah crosses to the dresser, collects a ledger and exits R, *giggling. It looks as though the charmed moment is lost between Lizzie and File)*

File *(moving to the door* R) Well . . .

Lizzie *(afraid he will leave)* What were we saying?

File. What were you sayin'?

Lizzie *(snatching for a subject that will keep him)* I—you were telling me about your divorce.

File. No—I wasn't—*(he studies Lizzie for a moment and changes his mind)* but I will. *(He moves* c) She walked out on me.

Lizzie. I'm sorry.

File. Yes—with a school-teacher. He was from Louisville.

Lizzie *(helping him get it said)* Kentucky?

(File *nods*)

Was she—I guess she was beautiful?

File (*with a step towards her*) Yes, she was.

Lizzie (*her hopes dashed*) That's what I was afr—(*she corrects herself*) that's what I thought.

File. Black hair.

Lizzie (*with an abortive little gesture to her un-black hair; drearily*) Yes—black hair's pretty, all right.

File. I always used to think—if a woman's got pitch-black hair she's already halfway to bein' a beauty.

Lizzie (*agreeing; but without heart*) Oh, yes—at least halfway.

File (*suddenly and intensely, like a dam bursting*) With a school-teacher, dammit! Ran off with a school-teacher.

Lizzie. What was he like?

(File *turns the chair* L *of the table and sits*)

File (*with angry intensity*) He had weak hands and near-sighted eyes—and he always looked like he was about ready to faint. And she ran off with him. And there I was . . .

Lizzie (*gently*) Maybe the teacher needed her and you didn't.

File. Sure I needed her.

Lizzie. Did you tell her so?

File (*raging*) No, I didn't. Why should I?

Lizzie (*astounded*) Why should you? Why didn't you?

File. Look here. There's one thing I've learned. Be independent. If you don't ask for things—if you don't let on you need things—pretty soon you don't need 'em.

Lizzie (*desperately*) There are some things you always need.

File (*doggedly*) I won't ask for anything.

Lizzie. But if you had asked her, she might have stayed.

File. I know darn well she mighta stayed. The night she left she said to me: "File, tell me not to go. Tell me don't go."

Lizzie (*in wild astonishment*) And you didn't?

File. I tried—I couldn't.

Lizzie. Oh, pride . . .

File. Look, if a woman wants to go, let her go. If you have to hold her back—it's no good.

Lizzie. File, if you had to do it over again . . .?

File (*interrupting; intensely*) I still wouldn't ask her to stay.

Lizzie (*in a rage against him*) Just two words—"Don't go"—you wouldn't say them?

File. It's not the words. It's beggin'—and I won't beg.

Lizzie. You're a fool!

(*It is a slap in the face. A dreadful moment for an overly proud, stubborn man. A dreadful moment for* Lizzie. *It is a time for drastic measures, or he will go. Having failed with File on an honest, serious level,* Lizzie *seizes upon flighty falsity, as a mode of behaviour.*

Precipitously she becomes Lily Ann Beasley, the flibbertigibbet, and chatters, with false, desperate laughter. FILE *rises and moves up* LC)

Whatever am I doing—getting so serious with you, File? I shoulda known better—because whenever I do, I put my foot in it. Because bein' serious—that's not my nature. I'm really a happy-go-lucky girl—just like any other girl and I . . . (*She crosses to* R *of File, picks up the bowl of grapes from the table and hands it to him*) Would you like some grapes?

FILE (*quietly*) No, thank you.

LIZZIE (*giddily*) They're very good. And so purply and pretty. We had some right after supper. Oh, I wish you'd been here to supper. I made such a nice supper. I'm a good cook—and I just love cooking. I think there's only one thing I like better than cookin'—reading a book. (*She crosses to the settee and picks up her book*) Do you read very much?

FILE (*watching Lizzie as if she were a strange specimen*) No. Only legal circulars—from Washington.

LIZZIE (*moving to* L *of File; seizing on any straw to engage him in the nonsensical chit-chat*) Oh, Washington—I just got through readin' a book about him. What a great man! Don't you think Washington was a great man?

FILE (*dryly*) Father of our country. (*He puts the bowl on the table*)

LIZZIE. Yes—exactly. (*More like Lily Ann Beasley than ever*) Oh, my—what a nice tie. I just die for men in black silk bow ties.

FILE (*getting angry; quietly*) It ain't silk—it's celluloid.

LIZZIE. No! I can't believe it. It looks so real—it looks so real.

FILE (*significantly; like a blow*) It ain't real—it's fake.

LIZZIE (*unable to stop herself*) And when you smile—you've got the strongest white teeth.

FILE (*angrily*) Quit that!

LIZZIE (*stunned*) What . . .?

FILE (*raging*) Quit it! Stop sashayin' around like a dumb little flirt.

LIZZIE (*with a moan*) Oh, no . . .

FILE. Silk tie—strong white teeth! What you take me for? And what do you take yourself for?

LIZZIE (*in flight; in despair*) I was trying to—trying to . . .

FILE. Don't be so damn ridiculous! Be yourself.

(FILE *exits quickly* R. LIZZIE, *alone, is at her wits' end, humiliated, ready to take flight from everything, mostly from herself.*

H.C. *enters down the stairs*)

H.C. What happened, Lizzie?

(JIM *rushes in* R)

Jim. What'd he do—run out on you? What happened? (*He moves up* L)

(Noah *enters hurriedly* R)

Noah. I never seen a man run so fast. Where'd he go?

Lizzie (*to all of them; berserk*) My God, were you watching a show? Did you think it was lantern slides?

Jim. What'd he say?

Noah. What'd you say?

Lizzie. I didn't say anything. Not one sensible thing. I couldn't even talk to him.

H.C. But you were talkin'.

Lizzie (*sitting on the hassock*) No. I was sashaying around like Lily Ann Beasley. I was making a fool of myself. Why can't I ever talk to anybody?

H.C. Lizzie, don't blame yourself. It wasn't your fault.

Noah (*savagely*) No. It wasn't her fault—and it wasn't File's fault. (*He moves* C *and squares off at H.C.*) And you know damn well whose fault it was.

H.C. You mean it was mine, Noah?

Noah. You bet it was yours.

(Lizzie, *seeing a fight, rises and tries to head it off*)

Lizzie. Noah—Pop . . .

H.C. No. He's got to explain that.

(Starbuck *enters* R *and leans against the door frame, listening in silence*)

Noah (*accepting H.C.'s challenge*) I'll explain it all right. You been building up a rosy dream for her—and she's got no right to hope for it.

H.C. She's got a right to hope for anything.

Noah. No. She's gotta face the facts—and you gotta help her face them. Stop tellin' her lies.

H.C. (*moving up* R) I never told her a lie in my life.

Noah. You told her nothin' *but* lies. She's the smartest girl in the world. She's beautiful. And that's the worst lie of all. Because you know she's not beautiful. She's plain.

Jim. Noah, you quit that.

Noah (*whirling on Jim*) And you go right along with him. (*He whips around to Lizzie*) But you better listen to me. I'm the only one around here that loves you enough to tell you the truth. You're plain!

Jim (*violently*) Dammit, Noah—you quit it!

Noah (*to Lizzie*) Go look at yourself in the mirror—you're plain.

Jim. Noah! (*He hurls himself at Noah*)

(Noah *falls on to the chair* R *of the table, but the instant* Jim *gets*

D

to him, Noah *strikes out with a tough fist. It catches* Jim *hard and he goes reeling. He returns with murder in his eye, but* Noah *slaps him across the face, grabs him and forces him back to the table. There is a frenetic outburst from* H.C. *and* Lizzie)

H.C. }
Lizzie } *(together)* {Noah—Jim—stop it!
{Stop it, both of you—stop it!

(Starbuck *rushes forward and breaks* Noah *and* Jim *apart.* Jim, *out of Noah's grip, goes berserk, bent on killing Noah, but* Starbuck *holds him off*)

Jim *(through tears and rage)* Let me go, Starbuck—let me go.
Starbuck *(holding Jim down* c) Quit it, you damn fool—quit it.
Jim *(with a cry)* Let go!
Starbuck. Get outside! *(He releases Jim)* Now go on—get outside.
Jim *(weeping)* Sure—I'll get outside. I'll get outside and never come back.

(Jim, *with an outburst of tears, rushes out* R. Lizzie *crosses to the door* R)

Noah. The next time that kid goes at me, I'll—I'll . . .
Starbuck. The next time he goes at you, I'll see he has fightin' lessons.
Noah. Look, you—clear out of here.
Starbuck. No, I won't clear out. And while I'm here, you're gonna quit callin' that kid a dumb-bell—because he's not. He can take a lousy little hickory-stick—and he can see magic in it. But you wouldn't understand that—because it's not in your books.
Noah *(moving to the door* R) I said clear out!
Starbuck *(moving above Lizzie; he cannot be stopped)* And while I'm here, don't you ever call her plain. Because you don't know what's plain and what's beautiful.
Noah. Starbuck, this is family—it's not your fight.
Starbuck. Yes, it is. I been fightin' fellas like you all my life. And I always lose. But this time, by God, this time . . .

(Starbuck *reins himself in, then exits hurriedly* R)

(Off; calling) Jimmy.

(Noah *breaks the stillness with quiet deliberateness*)

Noah *(to Lizzie and H.C.)* I'm sorry I hit Jim—and I'll tell him so. But I ain't sorry for a single word I said to her.
H.C. *(angrily)* Noah, that's enough!
Noah *(intensely)* No, it ain't enough. *(To Lizzie)* Lizzie, you better think about what I said. Nobody's gonna come ridin' up here on a white horse. Nobody's gonna snatch you up in his arms

and marry you. You're gonna be an old maid. And the sooner you face it, the sooner you'll stop breakin' your heart.

(Noah *exits up the stairs. There is a silence*)

Lizzie (*in the doorway* R; *dully and half to herself*) Old maid . . .

H.C. (*moving to* L *of the table*) Lizzie, forget it. Forget everything he said.

Lizzie. No—he's right.

H.C. (*with a plea*) Lizzie . . .

Lizzie. He's right, Pop. I've known it a long time. But it wasn't so bad until he put a name to it. Old maid. (*With a cry of despair*) Why is it so much worse when you put a name to it?

H.C. Lizzie, you gotta believe me . . .

Lizzie. I don't believe you, Pop. You've been lying to me—and I've been lying to myself.

H.C. Lizzie, honey—please . . .

Lizzie (*crossing to the chest*) Don't—don't. I've got to see things the way they are. And the way they will be. I've got to start thinking of myself as an old maid. Jim will get married. And one of these days, even Noah will get married. I'll be the visiting aunt. I'll bring presents to their children—to be sure I'm welcome. And Noah will say: "Junior, be kind to your Aunt Lizzie—her nerves aren't so good." And Jim's wife will say: "She's been visiting here a whole week now—when'll she ever go?" (*With an outcry*) Go where, for God's sake—go where?

H.C. (*in pain for her*) Lizzie, you'll always have a home. This house'll be yours.

Lizzie (*crossing to the stairs; hysterically*) House—house—house.

H.C. (*moving to* R *of Lizzie; trying to calm and comfort her*) Lizzie, stop it.

Lizzie. Help me, Pop—tell me what to do. Help me.

H.C. Lizzie—Lizzie!

Lizzie, *in a frantic movement, snatches up the quilt, and races out* R *as—*

the Lights *fade to* Black-Out

The Lights *come up on the tack-room* L, *leaving the living-room and the office in darkness. Bright moonlight alone illuminates the inside of the tack-room.* Starbuck *is preparing to go to bed. He takes off his boots and his neckerchief, then he stands* C *of the room, not moving but thinking intently. He arranges some feed sacks on the floor. It is stifling hot. He removes his shirt and sits on the edge of the buggy seat, suffering the heat. He waves his shirt around to make a breeze, rises, opens the door, then lies on the sacks. The stillness is a palpable thing, and the heat. As he relaxes, as he slips back into his solitude, a lonely little humming comes from him. It grows in volume and occasionally we hear the words of the song. Suddenly he hears a sound and sits bolt upright.*

STARBUCK (*calling*) Who's that? (*He rises tautly*) Who's there?

(LIZZIE *appears at the door, trying not to look into the room. She carries the quilt*)

LIZZIE (*trying to sound calm*) It's me—Lizzie.

(STARBUCK *puts on his shirt. There is an awkward moment, then* LIZZIE, *without entering the room, holds out the quilt*)

Here.

STARBUCK. What's that?

LIZZIE. Bed stuff—take it.

STARBUCK (*taking the quilt*) Is that what you came out for? (*He tosses the quilt on to the sacks*)

LIZZIE (*after a painful moment*) No—I came out, because . . . (*She finds it too difficult to continue*)

STARBUCK (*gently*) Go on, Lizzie.

LIZZIE (*with a step into the room*) I came out to thank you for what you said to Noah.

STARBUCK. I meant every word of it.

LIZZIE. What you said about Jim—I'm sure you meant that.

STARBUCK. What I said about you?

LIZZIE. I don't believe you.

STARBUCK. Lizzie! What are you scared of?

LIZZIE. You. I don't trust you.

STARBUCK. Why? What don't you trust about me?

LIZZIE. Everything. The way you talk, the way you brag— why, even your name.

STARBUCK. What's wrong with my name?

LIZZIE. It sounds fake. It sounds like you made it up.

STARBUCK. You're darn right. I did make it up.

LIZZIE. There! Of course.

STARBUCK. Why not? You know what name I was born with? Smith. Smith, for the love of Mike, Smith! Now what kind of a handle is that for a fella like me. I needed a name that had the whole sky in it. And the power of a man. Star—buck! Now there's a name—and it's mine.

LIZZIE. No, it's not. You were born Smith—and that's your name.

STARBUCK. You're wrong, Lizzie. The name you choose for yourself is more your own than the name you were born with. And if I was you I'd sure choose another name than Lizzie.

LIZZIE. Thank you—I'm very pleased with it.

STARBUCK. Oh, no, you ain't. You ain't pleased with anything about yourself. And I'm sure you ain't pleased with "Lizzie".

LIZZIE. I don't ask you to be pleased with it, Starbuck, I am.

STARBUCK. Lizzie! Why, it don't stand for anything.

LIZZIE. It stands for me. Me! I'm not the Queen of Sheba—I'm not Lady Godiva—I'm not Cinderella at the Ball.

STARBUCK. Would you like to be?

LIZZIE. Starbuck, you're ridiculous!

STARBUCK. What's ridiculous about it? Dream you're somebody—be somebody. But Lizzie—that's nobody. So many millions of wonderful women with wonderful names. (*In an orgy of delight*) Leonora, Desdemona, Caroline, Annabella, Florinda, Christina. (*With a pathetic little lift of his shoulders*) Lizzie!

LIZZIE (*turning to go*) Good night, Starbuck.

STARBUCK (*with a sudden inspiration*) Just a minute, Lizzie—just one little half of a minute.

(LIZZIE *stops and turns*)

I got the greatest name for you—the greatest name—just listen. (*Like a love lyric*) "Melisande."

LIZZIE (*flatly*) I don't like it.

STARBUCK. That's because you don't know anything about her. But when I tell you who she was—lady, when I tell you who she was!

LIZZIE. Who?

STARBUCK. She was the most beautiful—she was the beautiful wife of King Hamlet. Ever hear of him?

LIZZIE (*giving him rope*) Go on—go on.

STARBUCK. He was the fella who sailed across the ocean and brought back the Golden Fleece. And you know why he did that? Because Queen Melisande begged him for it. I tell you, that Melisande—she was so beautiful and her hair was so long and curly—every time he looked at her he just fell right down and died. And this King Hamlet, he'd do anything for her—anything she wanted. So when she said: "Hamlet, I got a terrible hankerin' for a soft Golden Fleece," he just naturally sailed right off to find it. And when he came back—all bleedin' and torn—he went and laid that Fleece of Gold right down at her pretty white feet. And she took that fur piece and she wrapped it around her pink naked shoulders and she said: "I got the Golden Fleece—and I'll never be cold no more." Melisande. What a woman! What a name!

LIZZIE (*forlornly*) Starbuck, you silly jackass. You take a lot of stories—that I've read in a hundred different places—and you roll them up into one big fat ridiculous lie.

STARBUCK (*angry and hurt*) I wasn't lyin'—I was dreamin'.

LIZZIE. It's the same thing.

STARBUCK. If you think it's the same thing, then I take it back about your name. Lizzie—it's just right for you. I'll tell you another name that would suit you—Noah. Because you and your brother—you've got no dream.

LIZZIE (*with an outcry*) You think all dreams have to be your kind. Golden Fleece and thunder on the mountain. But there are other dreams, Starbuck. Little quiet ones that come to a woman when she's shining the silverware and putting moth flakes in the closet.

STARBUCK. Like what?

LIZZIE. Like a man's voice saying: "Lizzie, is my blue suit pressed?" And the same man saying: "Scratch between my shoulder blades." And kids laughing and teasing and setting up a racket. And how it feels to say the word "Husband." There are all kinds of dreams, Mr Starbuck. Mine are small ones—like my name—Lizzie. But they're real like my name—real. So you can have yours—and I'll have mine. (*She is unable to control her tears*)

(STARBUCK *grabs Lizzie and holds her close*)

STARBUCK. Lizzie . . .

LIZZIE. Please . . .

STARBUCK. I'm sorry, Lizzie. I'm sorry.

LIZZIE. It's all right.

STARBUCK. I hope your dreams come true, Lizzie—I hope they do.

LIZZIE. They won't—they never will.

STARBUCK. Believe in yourself and they will.

LIZZIE. I've got nothing to believe in.

STARBUCK. You're a woman. Believe in that.

LIZZIE. How can I when nobody else will?

STARBUCK. You gotta believe it first. (*Quickly*) Let me ask you, Lizzie—are you pretty?

LIZZIE (*with a wail*) No—I'm plain.

STARBUCK. There! You see? You don't know you're a woman.

LIZZIE. I am a woman. A plain one.

STARBUCK. There's no such thing as a plain woman. Every real woman is pretty. They're all pretty in a different way—but they're all pretty.

LIZZIE. Not me. When I look in the looking glass . . .

STARBUCK. Don't let Noah be your lookin' glass. It's gotta be inside you. And then one day the lookin' glass will be the man who loves you. It'll be his eyes maybe. And you'll look in that mirror and you'll be more than pretty—you'll be beautiful.

LIZZIE (*crying out*) It'll never happen.

STARBUCK. Make it happen. Lizzie, why don't you think "pretty", and take down your hair? (*He reaches for her hair*)

LIZZIE (*in a panic*) No!

STARBUCK. Please, Lizzie. (*He takes the pins out of Lizzie's hair, and puts his arms around her*) Now close your eyes, Lizzie—close them.

(LIZZIE *closes her eyes*)

Now—say: I'm pretty.

LIZZIE (*trying*) I'm—I'm—I can't.

STARBUCK. Say it. Say it, Lizzie.

LIZZIE. I'm pretty.

STARBUCK. Say it again.

LIZZIE (*with a little cry*) Pretty.

STARBUCK. Say it—mean it.

LIZZIE (*exalted*) I'm pretty! I'm pretty! I'm pretty!

(STARBUCK *kisses* LIZZIE, *a long kiss, and she clings to him, passionately, the bonds of her spinsterhood breaking away. The kiss over, she collapses on the sacks, sobbing*)

(*Through her sobs*) Why did you do that?

STARBUCK (*kneeling beside her on the sacks*) Because when you said you were pretty, it was true.

(LIZZIE'S *sobs are louder, more heartrending because, for the first time, she is happy*)

Look at me.

LIZZIE. I can't.

STARBUCK (*turning her to him*) Stop cryin' and look at me. Look at my eyes. What do you see?

LIZZIE (*gazing through her tears*) I can't believe what I see.

STARBUCK. Tell me what you see.

LIZZIE (*with a sob of happiness*) Oh, is it me? Is it really me?

LIZZIE *goes to Starbuck with all her giving as—*

the CURTAIN *falls*

ACT III

Scene—*The living-room.*

When the Curtain *rises, the* Lights *come up on the living-room, leaving the office and tack-room in darkness.* H.C. *is speaking on the telephone.*

H.C. (*into the telephone*) Thank you, Howard—I'm sorry I woke you up . . . Well, if you hear from Jimmy, you call me right away, will you? . . . No, nothin's wrong . . . Thank you. (*He replaces the receiver and paces worriedly to the door* R)

(Noah *enters down the stairs. He wears a dressing-gown. He has been unable to sleep a wink*)

Noah (*on the stairs; grumpily*) Jimmy home yet?
H.C. (*crossing to* C) Nope.
Noah. That dopey kid. It's near two o'clock.
H.C. Go back to sleep, Noah. Don't worry about him.
Noah. I ain't worryin' about him. I don't give a damn what happens to him.
H.C. Okay—fine.
Noah. Maybe he's at the Hopkinsons's—I'll call them. (*He moves to the telephone*)
H.C. I called them all. Nobody seen him. (*He sits* R *of the table*)
Noah. If you'da seen my side of this, it wouldn't of happened.
H.C. I see your side, Noah—I just ain't on your side.
Noah (*angrily*) Nobody is.

(Noah *exits up the stairs. The sound of a klaxon motor horn is heard off.*
     Noah *re-enters down the stairs.*
     Jim *enters* R *and stands in the doorway. He looks very cocky, very self-satisfied, ten feet taller than before. He is smoking an enormous cigar with an air of aloof grandeur. He struts majestically*)

Jim. Good e-ve-ning.
Noah. Where the hell you been?
Jim (*with a lordly gesture*) Out—out—out.
Noah (*crossing to* Jim) What's wrong with you? Are you drunk?
Jim (*with an air of superiority*) No, Big Brother, I ain't drunk. But if I cared to be drunk, I'd be goggle-eyed.
H.C. (*secretly amused*) Where'd you get the stogie, Jim?
Jim. It ain't a stogie. It's a Havana Panatella. Eighty-five cents. And it's a present.

NOAH. Who the hell gave it to you?

JIM. I-the-hell gave it to me—for bein' a big boy.

NOAH. You didn't tell us where you been.

JIM (*circling around the room*) I don't have to—but I will. I been out with my favourite girl. (*He takes a little red hat from his pocket, unfolds it, then sits astride the chair L of the table*) Snookie.

NOAH. You crazy, dumb little . . .

JIM (*with an even smile; warningly*) Uh-uh-uh-uh! Don't say "dumb" no more, Noah. Or I shall take this eighty-five cent Havana Panatella and I shall squash it right in your mean old face.

H.C. What happened, Jimmy?

NOAH. Can't you see what happened? He went ridin' with Snookie Maguire and she got him all hot up and then, by God, she trapped him. (*He sits on the chest*)

JIM. Big Brother, you got it all wrong.

NOAH. Don't lie to me, Jimmy Curry. The minute I stopped lookin' after you, you got yourself in trouble.

JIM. Noah, when I tell you what really happened, you're gonna split your breeches. We went ridin'—yep, that's right. We opened that Essex up and we went forty million miles an hour. And then we stopped that car and we got out and we sat down under a great big tree. And we could look through the branches and see the sky all full of stars—damn, it was full of stars. And I turned around and I kissed her. I kissed her once, I kissed her a hundred times. And while I was doin' that, I knew I could carry her anywhere—right straight to the moon. But all the time, I kept thinkin': Noah's gonna come along and he's gonna say, "whoa!" But Noah didn't show up—and I kept right on kissin'. And then somethin' happened. She was cryin' and I was cryin' and I thought any minute now we'll be right up there on the moon. And then—then—without Noah bein' there—all by my smart little self—I said "Whoa!"

H.C. (*rising and moving to L of Jim*) Yippeeeee!

JIM (*formally*) Thank you, Pop—your yippee is accepted.

NOAH (*rising and moving C*) I don't believe a word of it. Why'd she give you the hat?

JIM (*rising*) For the same reason I gave her my elk's tooth. We're engaged.

NOAH (*moving RC*) So I was right. She did trap you.

JIM (*warningly*) Noah, I see I'm gonna have to give you this Havana Panatella.

H.C. Don't listen to him, Jimmy. Congratulations! (*He shakes hands with Jim*)

JIM (*touched*) Thanks, Pop—thank you very kindly. (*He crosses to the stairs. Suddenly elated*) I gotta tell Lizzie. Where's Lizzie?

NOAH. Where the Sam Hill do you think she is? She's asleep.

JIM (*moving up the stairs*) Well, then, I'll wake her up.

H.C. (*moving to the window up* c) Wait, Jimmy—Lizzie's not up there.

Jim. Where is she?

(*There is a pause*)

Noah. You mean with Starbuck?

H.C. Yes.

Jim. Boy, that's great! (*He pulls a cigar from his pocket*) I got another cigar for Lizzie.

Noah (*moving up* rc; *quietly to H.C.*) Wait a minute. You mean you let her walk in on that fella when he's sleepin'? You didn't even try to stop her?

H.C. No, I didn't. You called her an old maid. You took away the last little bit of hope she ever had. And when you left, she lifted up those bed linens and ran out. I didn't ask her where she was goin'—but I'm glad she went. Because if she lost her hope in here—maybe she'll find it out there.

Noah. That was in your mind the minute you laid eyes on that fella.

H.C. You put it awful cut and dried, Noah.

Noah. It's the truth.

Jim. Well, what of it? I think it's great them bein' out there together. They might get real serious about each other. And before you know it, I got me a new brother. Boy, I'd swap him for you any day.

Noah (*crossing and standing up* l) You won't have to swap him for anybody. Because he ain't the marryin' kind—not that faker.

Jim (*crossing to* c) I bet he is the marryin' kind—I bet he is. Hey, Pop, what do you figure a rainmaker makes?

H.C. (*soberly*) Don't let's be before-hand, Jimmy. (*He moves up* rc)

(File *and the* Sheriff *appear outside the door.* File *knocks on the door frame*)

File. Mind if we come in, H.C.?

H.C. Hello, File—Hey, Sheriff—come on in.

(File *and the* Sheriff *come into the room*)

Noah⎫(*together*) ⎰Hey, File.
Jim ⎭   ⎱Hey, Sheriff.

H.C. Kinda late to be visitin', ain't it, Sheriff?

Sheriff. Well, we're not exactly visitin', H.C.

File. How's Lizzie?

H.C. Fine, boy, fine. (*With a trace of puzzled amusement*) You just seen her a little while ago.

File (*with a little embarrassment*) Yeah—I know.

H.C. (*crossing to the settee*) You and the Sheriff come callin' on Lizzie?

FILE (*quickly*) No—uh—no.

H.C. (*picking up the newspaper from the settee*) What can I do for you? (*He sits on the settee*)

FILE (*moving* c) I'll tell you, H.C.

(JIM *crosses and sits on the stairs*)

We been gettin' a lot of phone calls from Pedleyville and Peak's Junction, and all down the state line. They been lookin' for a fella—well, he's a kinda con man. Name of Tornado Johnson. (*He cannot get his mind off Lizzie*) She asleep?

H.C. (*good-naturedly baiting File*) Who—Lizzie?

FILE. Well, I reckon she is. You get any wind of him?

H.C. Who?

FILE (*irritably*) Tornado Johnson.

II.C. Nope.

FILE (*taking a "Wanted" circular from his pocket*) Tornado Johnson—alias Bill Harmony—alias Bill Smith.

H.C. I never met anybody called himself by any of those names.

FILE. Anybody else come around here?

H.C. (*smiling*) Yep. You, File.

FILE (*looking towards the stairs*) Kind of a hot night to be asleep, ain't it?

H.C. Lizzie's a good sleeper.

FILE. Yeah—must be.

SHERIFF. No Tornado Johnson, huh?

H.C. Nope.

SHERIFF (*crossing to the chest and sitting*) Seems a little fishy.

JIM. How do you mean—fishy?

SHERIFF. Well, Pedleyville and the Junction and Three Point —we all kinda figured this together and—uh . . . (*Embarrassed, he looks at File*)

FILE. Look, H.C., we know it ain't like you to protect a criminal.

NOAH (*quickly*) Really a criminal, huh?

FILE (*uncomfortably*) Well, he's wanted.

H.C. What's he wanted for, File?

FILE (*referring to the circular*) He's wanted in the state of Kansas. He sold four hundred tickets to a big Rain Festival. No rain, no festival.

SHERIFF. In a small town in Nebraska, he drummed up a lot of excitement about what he called a Spectacular Eclipse of the Sun—and he peddled a thousand pair of smoked eyeglasses to see it with. No eclipse.

FILE. In the month of February he sold six hundred wooden poles. Called them Tornado Rods. Claimed that if that town ever got hit by a tornado the wind would just blow through there like a gentle spring breeze—and not hurt a thing. Well, when he left, the town got hit by every blow you can imagine—wind-storm, hail-storm, cyclone and hurricane. Blew the Tornado Rods off the roof and blew the town off the map.

(NOAH *crosses above the table to* R *of it*)

JIM (*rising*) Did it ever get hit by a tornado?
FILE. No, it didn't.
JIM (*resuming his seat*) Well, that's all he guaranteed—that it wouldn't get hit by a tornado. And it didn't.
H.C. Don't sound like a criminal to me, File.
SHERIFF. No, he don't—but we gotta do somethin' about him —we ain't locked anybody up for three weeks.
H.C. (*with a smile*) Sorry, I can't help you, Sheriff.
FILE (*moving to the window up* R) I got a feelin' you can. They say this fella carries a great big brass drum wherever he goes. (*He indicates the drum down* R) Whose drum is that?
JIM. It's mine. I'm figurin' to be a drummer.
FILE. Who painted that big white arrow on the ground?
H.C. I did.
FILE. What do you figure to be, H.C.—a whitewash painter?
H.C. Maybe.
FILE (*with a step towards the door* R) Yeah? Whose wagon is that?

(*There is a silence*)

SHERIFF (*rising and moving to the door* R) Let's go have a look at that wagon, File.

(FILE *and the* SHERIFF *exit quickly* R. H.C. *rises and moves to the door* R)

NOAH (*moving* LC; *in an outburst*) Why'd you do that? Why the hell did you do that?
H.C. I don't know.
NOAH. Why didn't you tell them—straight out: "The fella you're looking for is in the tack-room with my daughter."
H.C. (*moving* RC) Because he's with my daughter.
NOAH (*with angry resolve*) All right. I didn't tell them you were lyin'—I stood by you. But I ain't standin' by you any more. (*He crosses towards the door* R)
H.C. Where you goin', Noah?
NOAH. I'm goin' out to the tack-room and bring her in.
H.C. Noah, wait!
NOAH. And I'm gonna bring him in, too.
H.C. He's a quick fella, Noah—and you're a little slow on your feet.
NOAH (*moving to the table*) I'll be quicker with this. (*He takes a revolver from the table drawer*)
H.C. (*angrily*) Put that down.

NOAH (*moving LC*) You want Lizzie out there with him? He's a swindler and a crook and I don't know what else.

H.C. I'll tell you what else, Noah—he's a man.

JIM. Pop's right. Gettin' married is gettin' married.

H.C. Jimmy, you always say the smart thing at a dumb time.

JIM. Well, I'm all for her gettin' married—I don't care who the fella is.

NOAH. Is that the way you think, Pop?

H.C. You know it's not the way I think.

NOAH (*moving C*) Then I'm goin'.

H.C. I said stay here.

NOAH (*raging*) It ain't right, Pop—it ain't right.

H.C. (*exploding*) Noah, you're so full of what's right, you can't see what's good. It's good for a girl to get married, sure—but maybe you were right when you said she won't ever have that. Well, she's gotta have somethin'. (*With desperate resolution*) Lizzie has got to have somethin'. Even if it's only one minute—with a man talkin' quiet and his hand touchin' her face. And if you go out there and shorten the time they have together—if you put one little dark shadow over the brightest time of Lizzie's life—I swear I'll come out after you with a whip. (*Quietly*) Now you give me that gun.

> There is a taut moment during which NOAH and H.C. confront each other in open hostility. NOAH is too righteously proud to give the revolver to H.C. yet not strong enough to defy him. At last, to give in without entirely losing face, he puts the revolver back in the table drawer as—

> the LIGHTS *fade to* BLACK-OUT

> The LIGHTS *come up on the tack-room L, leaving the living-room and office in darkness.* STARBUCK *and* LIZZIE *are sitting on the sacks, leaning against the buggy seat. They are quite intimately close, looking out through the open door at the bright expanse of sky.* LIZZIE *has the shine of moonlight over her face and this glow, meeting her inner radiance, makes her almost beautiful.*

STARBUCK. And I always walk so fast and ride so far I never have time to stop and ask myself no question.

LIZZIE. If you did stop, what question would you ask?

STARBUCK. Well—I guess I'd say: "Big Man, where you goin'?"

LIZZIE (*quietly*) Big Man, where are you going?

STARBUCK (*after an indecisive moment*) I don't know—I reckon I better kiss you again. (*He kisses her and they are close for a moment*) Didn't anybody ever kiss you before I did, Lizzie?

LIZZIE (*with a wan smile*) Yes—once.

STARBUCK. When was that?

LIZZIE. I was about twelve, I guess. There was a boy with freckles and red hair—and I thought he was the beginning of the world. But he never paid me any mind. Then one day he was standing around with a lot of other boys. And suddenly, he shot over to me and kissed me hard, right on the mouth. And for a minute I was so stirred up . . . But then he ran back to the other kids and I heard him say: "I'll kiss anything on a dare—even your old man's pig." So I ran home and up the back stairs and I locked my door and looked at myself in the mirror—and from that day on I knew I was plain.

STARBUCK. Are you plain, Lizzie?

LIZZIE (*looking at him; smiling*) No—I'm beautiful.

STARBUCK. You are—and when I leave here, don't you ever forget it.

LIZZIE (*reconciled to his ultimate going; a little sadly*) I'll try to remember—everything—you ever said.

(STARBUCK *rises restively. Somehow he is deeply disturbed, lonely. He walks to the door, his back to Lizzie, and looks out at the night. There is searching in his face, and yearning*)

STARBUCK (*in a little outcry*) Lizzie, I want—I want to live forever.

LIZZIE (*full of compassion*) I hope you do—wherever you are— I hope you do.

STARBUCK. You don't say that as if you think I'll ever get what I'm after.

LIZZIE (*gently*) I don't really know what you're after.

STARBUCK. I'm after a clap of lightnin'. I want things to be as pretty when I get them as they are when I'm thinkin' about them. (*He moves to Lizzie and kneels beside her*)

(LIZZIE *is hurt.* STARBUCK *seems to disparage the moment of realization they have had together*)

LIZZIE. I think they're prettier when you get them.

STARBUCK. No. Nothin's as pretty in your hands as it was in your head. There ain't no world near as good as the world I got up here—why?

LIZZIE. I don't know. Maybe it's because you don't take time to see it. Always on the go—here, there, nowhere. Runnin' away —keepin' your own company. Maybe if you'd keep company with the world . . .

STARBUCK (*doubtfully*) I'd learn to love it?

LIZZIE. You might—if you saw it real. Some nights I'm in the kitchen washing the dishes, and Pop's playing poker with the boys. Well, I'll watch him real close. And at first I'll just see an ordinary middle-aged man—not very interesting to look at. And then, minute by minute, I'll see little things I never saw in him before. Good things and bad things—queer little habits I never noticed he had. And suddenly I know who he is—and I love him so much I could cry. And I want to thank God I took the time to see him real.

STARBUCK (*breaking out*) Well, I ain't got the time.

LIZZIE. Then you ain't got no world—except the one you make up in your head.

(*There is a long pause. When at last* STARBUCK *speaks it is with painful difficulty*)

STARBUCK (*rising*) Lizzie—I got somethin' to tell you—you were right—I'm a liar and a con man and a fake. (*He pauses. The words tear out of him*) I never made rain in my life—not a single raindrop—nowhere—not anywhere at all.

LIZZIE (*in a compassionate whisper*) I know.

STARBUCK. All my life—wantin' to make a miracle. Nothin'. I'm a great big blowhard.

LIZZIE (*gently*) No—you're all dreams. And it's no good to live in your dreams.

STARBUCK. It's no good to live outside them either.

LIZZIE. Somewhere between the two . . .

STARBUCK. Yes. Lizzie, would you like me to stick around for a while?

LIZZIE (*unable to stand the joy of it*) Did I hear you right?

STARBUCK. Not for good, understand—just for a few days.

LIZZIE (*rising*) You're—you're not fooling me, are you, Starbuck?

STARBUCK. No—I mean it.

LIZZIE (*crying*) Would you stay? Would you?

STARBUCK. A few days—yes.

LIZZIE (*her happiness bursting*) Oh! Oh, my goodness. Oh!

STARBUCK. Lizzie . . .

LIZZIE. I can't stand it—I just can't stand it.

STARBUCK (*taking her in his arms*) Lizzie . . .

LIZZIE. You look up at the sky and you cry for a star. You know you'll never get it. And then one night you look down—and there it is—shining in your hand.

LIZZIE, *half laughing, half crying, goes into* STARBUCK'S *arms as—*

the LIGHTS *dim to* BLACK-OUT

The LIGHTS *come up on the living-room, leaving the office and tack-room in darkness.* NOAH *and* H.C. *are waiting for things to come to pass.* NOAH *is seated* L *of the table, working at his ledgers.* H.C. *is seated on the chest. There is a restless tension in the room.* LIZZIE *enters* R. *The moonlight still glows on her.* NOAH *and* H.C. *turn, their eyes fixed on* LIZZIE, *who looks from one to the other, trying to contain the rhapsody in her.*

NOAH (*rising*) Where's Starbuck?

LIZZIE. In the tack-room. (*Unable to speak in front of Noah, she shifts nervously*) You know—I think I saw a wisp of a cloud—(*her happiness bursts forth*) no bigger than a mare's tail.

NOAH. She's talking like him.

LIZZIE (*sitting R of the table*) Yes, I am—yes.

NOAH. Whyn't you comb your hair?

LIZZIE (*with an excited laugh*) I like it this way. I'm going to wear it this way all my life. I'm going to throw away my pins. (*She takes a handful of hairpins from her pocket, rises and tosses the pins high in the air*) There! I've got no more pins. (*To H.C. In a rush*) But I've got something else.

H.C. (*quietly*) What, Lizzie?

LIZZIE. Pop—oh, Pop, I've got me a beau.

H.C. (*trying to smile; heavily*) Have you, honey?

LIZZIE. Not an always beau—but a beau for meanwhile. Until he goes. He says he'll go in a few days—but anything can happen in a few days—anything can happen. (*She moves to the door R; ecstatically*) Oh, Pop, the world's turned clear around.

NOAH (*after a pause*) Why don't you tell her, Pop?

LIZZIE. Tell me what?

H.C. (*with difficulty*) Lizzie, you were right about that fella. He's a liar and a con man.

LIZZIE (*with a cry*) But there's nothing bad about him, Pop. (*She runs to H.C. and kneels beside him*) He's so good—and so alone —he's so terribly alone.

NOAH (*rising and moving to the window up C; not unkindly*) Lizzie —come here.

LIZZIE. What?

NOAH. Look out this window.

(LIZZIE *rises, crosses to the window and looks out. A moment of bewilderment and dread*)

LIZZIE. What are they here for? What are they doing on his wagon?

(NOAH *turns away*)

Pop!

H.C. (*rising and moving C*) They're gettin' evidence against him, Lizzie. The Sheriff's here to lock him up.

LIZZIE. No! (*She moves towards the door R*)

NOAH (*detaining Lizzie*) Stay here, Lizzie.

LIZZIE. Let me go, Noah. (*To H.C. In a panic*) They've got no right to arrest him.

H.C. Yes, they have.

LIZZIE. Pop, we've got to help him.

H.C. (*painfully*) Lizzie, quit it. There's nothing we can do for him.

LIZZIE. Not for him—for me.

H.C. (*moving to* R *of Lizzie*) For you, Lizzie? I don't think he knows who you are. I think he dreamed you up in his head.

LIZZIE. No. He sees me as real as you do.

H.C. Do you believe that, Lizzie? Do you think he sees you real?

(LIZZIE *hesitates*)

Answer me.

LIZZIE (*after a painful pause*) Yes, he does.

H.C. All right, then—you better help him get away. (*He crosses to the settee and sits*) Go out the back door, and . . .

(LIZZIE *crosses towards the kitchen*)

NOAH. You're not gonna let her do that, Pop. (*He crosses towards the kitchen*)

H.C. Yes, I am.

NOAH. No. I won't let you. (*He bars the way to the kitchen*)

(LIZZIE, *in a wild flight, crosses to the door* R.

FILE *and* JIM *enter* R, *blocking the doorway. There is a taut moment*)

FILE. Well—you awake?

LIZZIE. Hello, File.

FILE. They said you were asleep.

LIZZIE. Did they? (*She tries to get past File*) Excuse me.

FILE (*blocking her path*) Where you goin', Lizzie?

LIZZIE (*afraid of giving Starbuck away*) Nowhere. Outside.

FILE (*suspiciously*) Wait a minute, Lizzie. What are you in such a rush for?

LIZZIE (*moving above the table; confused*) I—I just wanted to see what you were doing out there—on that wagon.

FILE. Well, I came in now. So you don't have to go out. (*Shrewdly and quickly*) Unless there's some other reason, for you goin'?

LIZZIE. No—no.

FILE (*to the others; his eye on Lizzie*) I guess we got what we came for. All right, H.C.—where is he? (*He moves up* RC)

H.C. Do your own work, File.

FILE. H.C., I don't want this family mixed up in trouble. Tell me where he is—please.

JIM. He left about an hour ago.

FILE. Where'd he go?

JIM. Pedleyville.

FILE. How'd he go? His wagon's still here.

H.C. He took Jim's roan.

JIM. Yeah—he took my roan.

FILE. I think you're lying—all of you. (*With sudden enraged*

E

exasperation) What the hell's goin' on here, anyway? I ask you questions and you tell me a pack of lies. (*He paces up and down* RC, *then moves to Lizzie*) And for what? A stranger. A man who don't mean anything to you. (*Abruptly he stands still as a thought assails him*) Or does he? (*As he feels the tautness of the silence, his attention slowly turns to Lizzie. He places himself squarely in front of her*) Maybe you better answer that question, Lizzie.

(*It is too much for* LIZZIE. *She takes a quick step towards the door in flight, but* FILE *grabs her*)

No—wait a minute. They said you were asleep—but you weren't. Why did they lie about that? Where were you, Lizzie?

LIZZIE (*painfully*) It has nothing to do with you.

FILE (*impulsively; with deep feeling*) It's got a lot to do with me. Tell me.

(STARBUCK *is heard approaching, singing at the top of his voice. There is a quick, sharp stir in the room.* LIZZIE *runs to the window up* C)

LIZZIE (*shouting desperately*) Starbuck—go away—run.

(STARBUCK *continues singing*)

(*Wildly*) Starbuck—run.

(NOAH *moves down* L.
STARBUCK *enters* R, *still singing. His pace is so rapid that he comes full into the room.* FILE *slams the door shut and Starbuck is confronted with* FILE's *drawn gun.* H.C. *rises*)

(*To Starbuck*) I told you to run.

STARBUCK. What's goin' on?

FILE. Sheriff! You're under arrest.

(STARBUCK *moves towards the kitchen*)

Don't go for that door.

(STARBUCK *stops and turns*)

LIZZIE. If you hadn't been singing, you'd have heard me.

STARBUCK. I never regret singin'. All right, Sheriff, let's go.

LIZZIE (*in an outcry*) File, wait a minute—let him go.

FILE. What?

LIZZIE. Let him get away.

FILE. I can't do that, Lizzie. (*He shows her the circular*) Look at this bulletin.

H.C. (*moving up* LC; *suddenly*) We don't have to look at that. We've been looking at him.

FILE. This is all I have to go by, H.C.

JIM (*moving down* RC) You've got us to go by, File. We spent the whole evenin' with this fella.

H.C. We gave him a hundred dollars—and we'll never regret a nickel of it.

JIM. He's not a criminal.

H.C. He don't belong in jail.

FILE (*with a sense of being stampeded*) Now, wait a minute!

LIZZIE. We took a chance with him, File. Now you take a chance with us.

STARBUCK (*moving* C) Give up, folks. A Sheriff's a Sheriff——and he can't see any further than his badge.

(FILE *flinches and* LIZZIE *hurries to him*)

LIZZIE (*confronting him squarely*) Is that true, File?

FILE. You know damn well it's not true.

LIZZIE. Then let him go.

JIM. Please let him go.

FILE (*looking at Noah; after the smallest instant*) Haven't heard a word from you, Noah. There'd be a lot of people around here who'd think I was breakin' the law. Right?

NOAH (*after a struggle with himself*) Nobody I know of. (*He sits on the stairs*)

FILE (*to Starbuck; quickly*) All right, get goin'. Get out of here. (*He moves to the chest and sits*)

STARBUCK. Well, I'm a son of a gun! (*He rushes to the door* R, *and stops on the threshold*)

FILE. Hurry up before I change my mind.

STARBUCK (*desperately*) Lizzie—it's as lonely as dyin' out there—will you come with me?

LIZZIE (*moving* RC; *amazed and unable to handle the sudden offer*) Starbuck . . .

STARBUCK. I'm talkin' to you, Lizzie. Come on.

(LIZZIE *takes a step towards Starbuck, tentative and frightened. Suddenly, out of the tense stillness, comes* FILE's *voice. The words he was never able to say, tear out of him in a tortured cry*)

FILE. Lizzie—don't go!

(LIZZIE *turns and looks at File, stunned and unable to believe it is File's voice*)

LIZZIE. What—what did you say?

FILE. I said, "Don't go."

LIZZIE. Oh, what'll I do?

STARBUCK. Hurry up, Lizzie—please.

(LIZZIE, *caught between the two men, glances wildly around the room*)

LIZZIE. Pop, what am I going to do?

H.C. (*moving* LC) Whatever you do, remember you been asked. You don't never have to go through life a woman who ain't been asked.

E*

STARBUCK. I'm sure askin'. Lizzie, listen. You're beautiful now, but you come with me and you'll be so beautiful, you'll light up the world.

LIZZIE (*frightened*) No—don't say that.

STARBUCK (*he cannot be stopped*) You'll never be Lizzie no more —you'll be—you'll be Melisande.

LIZZIE (*with a cry that is part lament, part relief*) Oh, Starbuck, you said the wrong thing.

FILE (*rising*) Melisande? What the hell does that mean? Her name's Lizzie Curry.

STARBUCK. It's not good enough—not for her.

FILE. It's good enough for me.

LIZZIE. No—I've got to be Lizzie. Melisande's a name for one night—but Lizzie can do me my whole life long. (*She turns away from Starbuck. Her decision has been made*)

(STARBUCK *tries to hide his deep desperation. He tries to smile, to be the braggart again. He addresses the Curry men with a bravura shout*)

STARBUCK. Well, boys, I'm sorry about the rain—but then I didn't stay my full time. So there's your hundred dollars. (*He tosses the bundle of notes up in the air*)

(JIM *catches the bundle of notes, then sits on the chest*)

Another day, maybe—in a dry season. So long, folks.

(STARBUCK *exits* R *in a streak of dust.* H.C. *crosses to the door* R)

LIZZIE. Thank you, File, thank you.

FILE (*studying her*) Well! You've got your hair down.

JIM. Yep! She sure has changed.

(FILE *takes a step towards* LIZZIE. *They look closely at each other. He smiles, the first full, radiant smile we have seen on his face. And the warmth of it shines on* LIZZIE *and she smiles also. Suddenly, in the distance, there is a quick, low rumble of thunder*)

NOAH (*without looking at Jim*) Jimmy, for Pete sake, stop beatin' that drum.

JIM. I ain't beatin' no drum.

(*The others look at Jim. Another rumble of thunder is heard off*)

H.C. (*unable to believe what he hears*) That sounds like . . . (*With a shout*) It's thunder!

(*A streak of lightning flashes, dimming the room and electrifying it at the same time*)

JIM (*rising*) Lightning!

H.C. Light-ning!

FILE. Look at it! It's gonna rain!

Jim. He said twenty-four hours—he said twenty-four hours.

(*The lightning flashes and there is a roll of thunder*)

Lizzie (*in highest exaltation*) It's going to rain! Rain!

(Starbuck *suddenly appears at the door* R, *with a look of glory on his face*)

Starbuck. Rain, folks—it's gonna rain. Lizzie—for the first time in my life—rain. (*He moves to Jim*) Gimme my hundred dollars.

(Jim *joyously hands the bundle of notes to Starbuck*)

(*He rushes to the door* R *and turns to Lizzie*) So long—beautiful!

Starbuck *rushes out* R *as—*

the Curtain *falls*

FURNITURE AND PROPERTY LIST

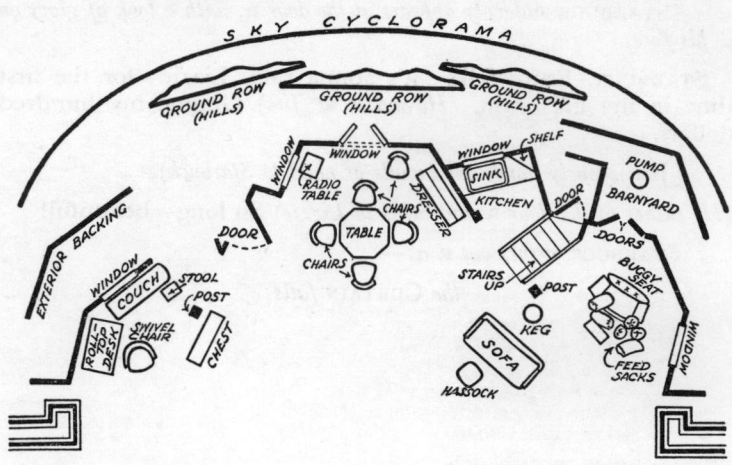

ACT I

The Living-room

On stage—In living-room: Dutch dresser. *On it:* 6 mugs, 6 plates, clock, check tablecloth, glass jar with knives, forks and spoons, ashtray, plate with bread, jam, sugar basin, cruet, dish with butter, tumblers, glass water jug

    In cupboard: 2 ledgers, pen, ink, draughts board and men

Dining-table. *In drawer:* revolver

5 chairs

Settee. *On it:* gifts, fountain pen, horsehair hat-band, tooled leather belt with large shiny buckle, H.C.'s hat

On floor by settee: gift wrappings

Behind settee: suitcase

Hassock

Linen chest. *In it:* quilt

On wall above door: clothes hooks

Table. *On it:* primitive crystal radio set hooked up to old phonograph horn

On wall R of window: calendar with pencil on string

Wall telephone

Oil lamp pendant

Oil lamp on bracket

In kitchen: sink

       frying pans and other cooking utensils

       water pitcher

       tea-cloth

       clean towel

On porch: large thermometer

In office: roll-top desk. *On it:* blotter, ink, pens, pencils, note-pads,
goose-neck lamp, ashtray, telephone, papers
In drawer: cigar box with needle and thread
swivel chair
stool
couch
bulletin board with notices
spittoon
clock
law books

In tack-room: wagon wheel
saddles
horse traces
sacks of feed
farm tools
buggy seat
nail keg
farm lantern

Off stage—Saddle (NOAH)
Shoes (JIM)
Jug of milk (H.C.)
Plate with two raw eggs (H.C.)
2 plates with scrambled eggs (H.C.)
Pot of coffee (NOAH)

Personal—NOAH: pocket watch

The Office

During Scene 2

Strike from living-room—everything from table
gifts and wrappings
suitcase

Set in living-room—On table: cloth, cutlery for five, 5 table napkins, 5 glasses,
cruet, glass bowl with fruit, pitcher of water

The Living-room

Off stage—Walking-stick (STARBUCK)

ACT II

The Living-room

Strike—Everything from table
Set—On table: cash-box, 100 dollars in notes
On dresser: book
On hassock: Starbuck's stick

Transfer ledger from chest to dresser

The Office

During Scene 2

Set—On porch: bundle of rag
On table: bowl of grapes

The Living-room

Off stage—Whitewash brush, pail of white paint (H.C.)
    Large brass drum and beater (JIM)

The Tack-room

Off stage—Quilt (LIZZIE)

ACT III

The Living-room

Set—*On settee:* newspaper
Off stage—2 cigars (JIM)
    Red hat (JIM)
    "Wanted" circular (FILE)

The Tack-room

During Scene 2
Set—*On table:* ledgers, pen, ink

The Living-room

Personal—STARBUCK: bundle of dollar notes
    SHERIFF: revolver
    FILE: revolver
    LIZZIE: hair-pins

LIGHTING PLOT

Property Fittings Required—goose-neck lamp, 2 farm lanterns, pendant oil lamp, oil lamp on bracket

Interior. The same scene throughout. A composite set with a living-room c, an office R and a tack-room L

THE MAIN ACTING AREA—covers the whole stage

THE APPARENT SOURCES OF LIGHT ARE—in daytime: in the living-room— a window back c, and a window up R; in the office—a window R; in the tack-room—a window L. At night: in the living-room—an oil lamp pendant c and an oil lamp on a bracket L; in the office—a goose-neck lamp; in the tack-room—a farm lantern

ACT I   The living-room. Early morning

Pre-set—Effect of blazing sunshine
    All fittings off

Cue 1   After rise of CURTAIN   (page 1)
    Bring up lights as pre-set for living-room. The office and tack-room in darkness

Cue 2   At end of Scene   (page 12)
    Dim all lights to BLACK-OUT

       The office

Pre-set—Effect of sunshine
    Fittings off

Cue 3   When ready
    Bring up lights as pre-set for office. The living-room and tack-room in darkness

Cue 4   At end of Scene   (page 17)
    Dim all lights to BLACK-OUT

       The living-room

Pre-set—Effect of sunset
    Fittings off

Cue 5   When ready
    Bring up lights as pre-set for living-room. The office and tack-room in darkness

ACT II   The living-room

Pre-set—Night effect
    All fittings on

Cue 6   After rise of CURTAIN   (page 26)
    Bring up lights as pre-set for living-room. The office and tack-room in darkness

Cue 7   At end of Scene   (page 31)
    Dim all lights to BLACK-OUT

       The office

Pre-set—Night effect
    Fittings on

Cue 8   When ready
            Bring up lights as pre-set for office. The living-room and tack-
            room in darkness

Cue 9   At end of Scene   (page 33)
            Dim all lights to BLACK-OUT

            The living-room

Pre-set—Night effect
            All fittings on

Cue 10   When ready
            Bring up lights as pre-set for living-room. The office and tack-room
            in darkness

Cue 11   At end of Scene   (page 47)
            Dim all lights to BLACK-OUT

            The tack-room

Pre-set—Bright moonlight effect
            Fittings off

Cue 12   When ready
            Bring up lights as pre-set for tack-room. The living-room and office
            in darkness

ACT III   The living-room

Pre-set—Night effect
            All fittings on

Cue 13   After rise of CURTAIN   (page 52)
            Bring up lights as pre-set for living-room. The office and tack-room
            in darkness

Cue 14   At end of Scene   (page 57)
            Dim all lights to BLACK-OUT

            The tack-room

Pre-set—Bright moonlight effect
            Fittings off

Cue 15   When ready
            Bring up lights as pre-set for tack-room. The living-room and
            office in darkness

Cue 16   At end of Scene   (page 59)
            Dim all lights to BLACK-OUT

            The living-room

Pre-set—Night effect
            All fittings on

Cue 17   When ready
            Bring up lights as pre-set for living-room. The office and tack-
            room in darkness

Cue 18   H.C.: "It's thunder."   (page 64)
            Flash of lightning

Cue 19   JIM: ". . . twenty-four hours."   (page 65)
            Flash of lightning

EFFECTS PLOT

ACT I

The Living-room

The Office

No cues

The Living-room

ACT II

The Living-room

The Office

The Living-room

The Tack-room

No cues

ACT III

The Living-room

Cue 16   NOAH: "Nobody is."   (page 52)
Sound of klaxon horn

The Tack-room

No cues

The Living-room

Cue 17   JIM: ". . . sure has changed."   (page 64)
Low rumble of distant thunder

Cue 18   JIM: ". . . beatin' no drum."   (page 64)
Rumble of thunder

Cue 19   JIM: ". . . twenty-four hours."   (page 65)
Rumble of thunder